Los Gatos High School

DISC

D0342768

EDITH JACKSON

Rosa Guy

Los Gatos High School

LAUREL-LEAF BOOKS

Published by
Dell Publishing
a division of
Bantam Doubleday Dell Publishing Group, Inc.
666 Fifth Avenue
New York, New York 10103

If you purchased this book without a cover you should be aware
that this book is stolen property. It was reported as "unsold and
destroyed" to the publisher and neither the author nor the
publisher has received any payment for this "stripped book."

To Dedier and Chief too

Copyright © 1978 by Rosa Guy

All rights reserved. No part of this book may be reproduced or
transmitted in any form or by any means, electronic or
mechanical, including photocopying, recording, or by any
information storage and retrieval system, without the written
permission of the Publisher, except where permitted by law.

The trademark Laurel-Leaf Library® is registered in the U.S.
Patent and Trademark Office.

The trademark Dell® is registered in the U.S. Patent and
Trademark Office.

ISBN: 0-440-21137-9

RL: 4.7.

Reprinted by arrangement with the author

Printed in the United States of America

February 1992

10 9 8 7 6 5 4 3 2 1

BC#24354

BOOK I
The Foster Family

ONE

"By the sweat of thy brow shall ye eat bread! Saith the Lord! And! He saith! Six days of the week shall ye toil! But on the seventh! The Sabbath! Give ye thanks unto the Lord! Now! He ain't said nothing 'bout jiving 'round sleeping off no Saturday night drunk! That ain't what he talking 'bout at all. . . ."

Reverend Jenkins talked loud. His big voice shook the little A.M.E. Zion church. His bushy eyebrows jutted out, quivering; his eyes stretched out of his head, trying to stare into the souls of us poor sinners. And I sat digging the dude across the aisle.

The dude looked like I felt. Twisting and turning, ready to take off. But like me he had to sit and listen, judging from the snatch Mrs. Bates had on him. She had him hooked, holding tight to his arm, forcing him to sit though his feet were making it in the aisle. Her wicked smile, her eyes laughing up at Reverend Jenkins, told that he had to sit.

The dude caught me staring and stared back. He

hunched his shoulders, pointed to the preacher, and put a hand under his chin, brushing a make-believe beard. He grinned.

Sure 'nough, the sweat pouring down the preacher's cheeks had rounded his chin, and one drop hung there, refusing to fall. I giggled. Then I turned to see if Mother Peters had heard. But sitting at the far end of the row, between plump, brown, twelve-year-old Bobby and tall Kenneth—the white one—she never glanced at me. I turned back to the sharp cat and found I had lost him.

He had turned to Mrs. Bates, trying to get loose from her hold, and although I kept looking, waiting for him to look back at me, he never did. Then he whispered something to Mrs. Bates. She laughed. My face jumped hot. I turned my head away. Dudes gave me pains in different places. I glanced down at my sisters, sitting between me and Kenneth, dressed in their Sunday best. None of us really cared about boys anyhow.

Thirteen-year-old Bessie, staring up at Reverend Jenkins—her eyes big under her red hat, her red plaid spring coat hiding her full bosom—never heard a word he said. She stayed solid in some other place. Who knew where? Bessie had always hidden her inner thing, and getting to be a teen hadn't changed that. She didn't dig boys special. Bessie went for people—and things—that went for her, including cats and dogs. One lick, one nudge, and they had her.

Minnie was only eleven and interested in books and—since coming to Peekskill and going to that almost-all-white school—her white friends. She sat there in her navy blue coat and white straw hat, her dark skin Vaselined down, which made her round nose shine to match her bright round eyes. I knew she was sucking in everything the preacher said, and we'd all hear it again—in her way—in her new "white"-sounding voice that got on my nerves. Which didn't take away from one straightening fact: Minnie was the brightest of us all. She had never had a bad mark since starting school, even though since becoming wards of The Institution, we had shed homes and schools like cats shed fur.

Suzy, ten months older than Minnie, had slid back to F marks—like me and Bessie. A couple of years ago Minnie had caught up with Suzy in school and had left her far behind. It had made Suzy no difference. All Suzy cared about was Minnie. She followed Minnie around, not giving one thought to boys. She even dressed like Minnie. And when I teased her about acting like Minnie's twin, trying to make her feel bad, Suzy paid me no mind. She only stuck closer to Minnie—her shadow.

Yet Suzy looked more like me than the other two did. She was plain, brown-skinned, with short, nappy hair that even hair straighteners didn't manage. But Suzy had long legs, and I knew they would push her far higher than my five feet three inches by the time she reached my age, seventeen.

I guess Suzy's looking like me made me want her to be smart on her own, do things I hadn't been able to, on account of having to look after all of them. No wa—ay. Suzy and Minnie had shared the same crib ever since Minnie was born. That had done it.

And me. I had no kinda time to think about dudes. I was too busy going to school, keeping my eyes on the kids, and while Mother Peters went out to her part-time job, seeing that her house routine kept going. It took all my time. Nope. No time for dudes. Yet I kept pulling at the skirt of my new dark-blue spring suit and fixing my white cotton blouse, to make sure I looked pressed, all the while straining not to look across the aisle.

But I kept seeing him in my mind. Mr. Brown, I called him, because of his brown blazer, brown pants, his tan turtleneck shirt, making his brown skin browner. He sure looked go—od. Looked like he belonged right there with Mrs. Bates.

"And He shall bring down His wrath!" Reverend Jenkins kept sounding off. "I say! He shall bring down His wrath! On those make-believers who think that they! Can take *His* day! As an excuse to rest after a night of SIN!"

"Amen! Brother! Amen!" Women in the congregation shouted agreement, nodded. Some fanned themselves or tapped their feet. "Mmmmm," others groaned. Heads bobbed. Kept bobbing. "Say it, Brother! Say it!"

A movement across the aisle told me that Mr. Brownman wanted my attention. He got it. He moved his finger in a circle out around his ear, then pointed to the preacher. He made another circle; this time he pointed to Mrs. Bates. Then he made a fist, kept raising it and kept bringing it down on his head—showing God's wrath come down upon him. I giggled. Loud. Mrs. Bates looked over at me. Smiled. I blushed. Turned away. This time I kept my head turned. Those eyes of Mrs. Bates had a way of burning through me.

A straightening fact: I thought Mrs. Bates the gonest: six feet tall, thin, with pretty teeth that shone when she did that slow pull back of her thick lips to the laugh lines at the sides of her mouth. She had mixed gray hair, bunned at her neck; always wore two-piece outfits of soft wool, in different colors, which seemed made to fit her long, lanky frame. And she always wore one strand of pearls. My name for her from the first: El-e-gant. I had a picture of her eyes drawn in my head: two pools of melted tar, beneath which the sun had sunk. I never looked straight into them. Whenever she caught me looking, I looked away, hot—embarrassed!

". . . and now I want to thank those brothers and sisters who came out to worship on this Sabbath. And to ask all of you to bring out your families, your friends, your neighbors. So that all of us may join hands and pray together for His divine blessing. Let us pray. . . ."

Services over. I moved to make time up the aisle. But Mother Peters gave me a sign. I had to wait for the row behind us to empty. I watched as long-legged Brown, looking like he wanted to climb over the backs of the rest of the congregation, made it out of that church.

TWO

Disappointed, I stood on the top step of the white frame church, looking all around. But Mr. Brown was not to be seen, not even at the corner where Mrs. Bates stood, surrounded by her tangle of followers. Mrs. Bates was a retired lawyer who made big noises in the community, and young folks were always trying to get near her. It sure meant something to be a black lawyer, even a retired one, in that small black community in Peekskill.

The early afternoon sun splattered over the tops of the surrounding houses, spilling warm rays over the lawns and down to the cool narrow street, where Mother Peters joined the group of women, settling themselves in their shadows, ready to carry on about the week's happenings. We six kids stood at the side of the church, watching the door, waiting for our friends. Mrs. Jenkins, the preacher's wife, strutted down hen-fashion and waddled over, in her sharp clothes, to snatch her ray of sunshine alongside Mother

Peters. Her two foster daughters, Diane, fifteen, and Elizabeth, seventeen, came to stand with us.

"Hey, Edith." Diane, always ready with the jokes, nudged me as the preacher's two *real* daughters followed their mother. "You want to see a sample of how not to cut a suit to hide the stretching skin?"

"Sure thing."

"Dig. Dig."

That made all eight of us stare at the two plump but well-dressed girls standing just a short distance away.

"I do declare . . ." Diane joked without one line creasing her tight skin, "when asses start making clothes—and ex-pensive—look like that, they ought to make laws against asses."

I cracked up. A real trick laughing loud enough for the girls to hear without bugging Mother Peters. But I hated the Jenkins daughters. They were light-brown-skinned—a cross between their black father and light-skinned mother. They never looked at us foster kids, not in school, not on the streets, not even in their own father's church. I had never ever seen them talking to their own foster sisters. "They sure do make a show," I said, nudging Diane on.

"Yeah, a dog show."

"Oh, I think they sharp," Bessie, her wide eyes mussing up, said. "They real down. I hear they even play the piano."

"Play!" Diane snorted. "Ha. You mean they practice. Them's two different things, baby. They been practicing since I got here six years ago. They still practicing. Dance too."

Diane stood on tiptoe, looking short and square. Then elbows at her sides, hands limp in front like paws, tipping in circles from side to side, she pretended to dance. We roared. "I tell you, that Miss Welk's Studio prepares folks for the circus. And all the while they simping, you know what Lizzie and me be doing?"

"What?"

"Washingdishesironingwashingdishesdryingdishes-
washingwindowsscrubbingfloorswashingdishes . . ."

Mrs. Jenkins walked up with her two daughters. She
stopped a second to look over our heads, then walked
on. Diane and Lizzie let them go on about ten paces
before falling in. Diane kept making signs at their
switching backsides, and Bobby, hating to be outdone,
ran up behind them, wiggling his broad behind.

"Bobby!" Mother Peters' voice snapped.

Just like that the laughing stopped and we fell into
pairs, me on one side and Bobby on the other, around
Mother Peters. Then came Bessie with Kenneth—the
white one—Minnie and Suzy behind them.

We looked good—as long as there were no folks like
the Jenkinses around to compare to: plain but proper.
Clean. Not expensive but not sloppy. I saw to that.
Mother Peters saw to it that I saw to that. We walked
proud, together—all of us foster children.

Which made me think of Lizzie. I looked back to
see her stooped figure keeping up with brisk-stepping
Diane on the narrow sidewalk. Funny about Lizzie.
She never talked. Sure, she laughed at Diane's clown-
ing. But I'd really never heard the sound of her talking
voice.

We walked down the block and had already turned
the corner when we heard Reverend Jenkins call.

"Sister Peters. Sister Peters." He ran up to us. "I
didn't want you to get away before I had a chance to
greet you. You know I always have to tell you how
proud I am when I see you on the Sabbath with these
poor children. You set such a good example for the
entire community."

Rubbing down our pride. He did it for meanness
because we walked together like a family instead of
trailing ten paces behind Mother Peters the way his
foster kids had to do behind him and his family.

"Thank you, Reverend Jenkins." Mother Peters
kept her smile working, her eyes behind her gold-

rimmed glasses blinking respectfully. "That's mighty kind of you."

A giant from close up, Reverend Jenkins' handsome, smooth blackness lost its godliness when he broadened his smile, exposing his double teeth, and he went right into evilness when his eyes settled on me. Like he got lost trying to find my soul and looked instead through my clothes to my naked flesh. A straightening fact: old Rev never saw the color of my eyes. And when he looked at me, my tongue just automatically reached back for the wad of gum I kept hidden and I got to chewing.

"Ye—es," he smiled. "Whenever I talk to Mrs. Brown at The Institution, I always say a good word for you and the work you are doing for these poor, unfortunate souls."

"Mrs. Brown's told me." Mother Peters' tight smile widened.

But if old Rev thought he'd pull an invitation out of Mother Peters with his jive-ass talk, he had another think coming. A straightening fact: Mother Peters did not want one living soul coming into her house, digging into her relations with Uncle Daniels. Uncle Daniels was our house secret.

"I want to thank you again, Reverend Jenkins," Mother Peters said. "You are indeed a very thoughtful man. We'll be seeing you next Sunday." Her thick-waisted, straight-backed body moved, determined to leave. But just then Mrs. Bates walked up.

"There you are, Reverend Jenkins, Mrs. Peters. I'm so glad to get a chance to talk to both of you. I hope I can inveigle you to join us Wednesday at a meeting at the library. The district leader will be there, as well as our congressman and most of the leading citizens. The discussion will be about our plans for a new wing in the library. I do—"

Mother Peters threw up her hands. "Of course I'd like to come, Mrs. Bates, but I have so much to do—

my part-time job—the children. Maybe I can send Edith? She is smart—"

"That's hardly the work for children, Mrs. Peters." Mrs. Bates's full lips rolled back to show her big white teeth. The sun under the black of her eyes caught mine. Mother Peters' smile shrank. Reverend Jenkins shifted from foot to foot. They sure didn't dig her.

"You know"—Mrs. Bates went on—"I checked up at her school and found that Edith is really far behind in her school work. If she is free Wednesday, my daughter Debra will be happy to go over some of her problems with her." Fumbling in her oversize bag, Mrs. Bates took out a card and handed it to me. "My address," she said, showing her even teeth again. But she had lost me.

Embarrassed! Imagine. Checking up on me! Calling me dumb out here in the street! My eyes kept sliding away from the kids—especially Bobby and Minnie. If I heard about this, I'd give it to them—but good. God, I hated her! I cut my eyes down to her feet, tried to work them up the length of her: tall, skinny, string bean of a witch! One more inch to her heels and I'd call her giraffe.

I waited for Mother Peters to gentle Mrs. Bates away, but that woman had made us all feel right stupid: Mother Peters, for thanking old Rev over us as well as for tricking her into saying I was free on Wednesday; Reverend Jenkins, for those big praises when he hadn't even bothered to check us out at school; and me, for liking a simple witch who went poking her nose where it didn't belong.

"Mrs. Bates." Reverend Jenkins' smile and his voice were real polite. "I do think that young man across the street is trying to get your attention."

There he was, Mr. Fine-Thing Brown, walking up and down like the sidewalk had become his cage. He kept cutting his eyes over at us, looking as mad as a polluted wind ready to fly over and contaminate us all.

"That's my nephew." Mrs. Bates turned her smile on Mr. Brown to cool him where he stood. "He came up from New York this morning, and I snatched him the minute he walked in. I swear to you he shall never forgive me."

Hooking her arm through the Reverend's, she drew him across the street, still talking. "Reverend, it is so important . . ."

I stood at the curb, looking as she opened her car door for her nephew. I saw him get in and sit down, his legs shaking in those brown pants, like he wanted to have a fit. She kept right on talking to Reverend Jenkins, and when he finally walked away, she got into the car and drove over to where I stood. "See you Wednesday, Edith," she called.

Hot, then cold, then hot, I kept my eyes hard on the two of them as they drove away. The car roared down the avenue, then skidded around a corner and out of sight. Still I stood there hating her. Thinking of those brown legs shaking and shaking. Mad at her. Mad at the world.

"Edith!"

I had to run almost the whole block to catch up. I fell in step with the family, still thinking of laughing black eyes and shaking brown legs. "Edith," Mother Peters scolded, "how many times must I tell you that it is not ladylike to chew gum?"

THREE

Mrs. Bates's going to my school to check me out kept me evil for the next two days. Gold-black eyes and pretty-teeth smile and being a lawyer—retired or not—didn't give her that right. And I didn't care what anyone said. I had no intention of going to her house on Wednesday.

At school I kept eye-balling the teachers, trying to see into the head of the one who had made it her business to put *my* business in the streets. Like it made a difference. In that special school for industrial courses, English and math were compulsory. And if I never learned to sew or to design, who cared? I was seventeen, ready to quit or be thrown out if I flunked. I'd still get work sewing in a factory.

At home that week the kids kept messing with my nerves. Tuesday night I heard them playing upstairs instead of studying. I went to the foot of the stairs and yelled up, "Y'all cut that crapping around and get to your homework."

14

For answer I heard giggles and scuffling around. "Did y'all hear what I said?" I shouted again. Made no sense my taking it out on the kids. But I wasn't in a mood to be made a fool of. "Get to work 'fore I come up there and go up side a your heads."

Like he was born to cross me, hardheaded Bobby ran out of the playroom to the top of the stairs and stood, his fat backsides turned to me, wiggling. "Whose head you going up side of? Ain't mine, I bet you."

I took two steps at a time and had almost caught him when he ran into the bedroom he shared with Kenneth. He slammed the door. Kenneth stood blocking my way, grinning. I glared at him. "Get outa my way, white boy. I ain't got no trouble with you."

The grin slid off Kenneth's face, and his blue eyes turned hard, serious. "Name is Kenneth," he said.

He was only fourteen, but he stood almost six feet. His shoulders were broad, and those clear blue eyes looked beyond caring about having to take me on. Mother Peters didn't allow us foster kids to abuse one another. It abused Kenneth to be called white.

Kenneth had run away from Catholic homes for boys, from white foster parents, and from any other place to do with white folks. Mother Peters had taken him in as a special favor to Mrs. Brown. He had been with Mother Peters for three years—two years longer than we had. Kenneth never called anybody except by their names—including me. So I backed down.

"Okay, Kenneth," I said. But my tongue had reached back into my mouth for my gum, and I laid down some hard chewing to prove to him that house rules had won. He kept his eyes dead on mine. I repeated, "Kenneth." He dropped his head and made it into the playroom.

I had no fight with Kenneth except that to me black folks and white folks didn't dig each other. In Harlem I never had anything to do with whites, except for teachers who didn't dig us. And it was no secret the hell white folks raised when black folks were bussed to their schools. So how come Kenneth rated a black foster mother?

I decided to go after spoiled Bobby. He was Mother Peters' favorite.

"Okay, brickhead," I called out, after going into the bedroom and not seeing him. He was hiding. "I'm counting to five. If you're still in here when I'm through, I'll lock this door, then it's me and you. Got it? One—two—three—four." I felt him brush past me, moving fast. I heard him scuttling across the hall. Cheers and laughs went up from inside the playroom.

I looked into this den that Mother Peters had made into a playroom, study, and library for us. Everybody was busy studying or pretending to be. Judy Cramer, Minnie's little white blond friend, sat huddled with Minnie and Suzy. Kenneth sat with Bessie and Bobby, still giggling, his head bowed deep in a book. Long as they were where I asked them to be, it made me no difference. I went down to the kitchen to wash the dinner dishes.

I loved washing dishes. Elbow-deep in suds, looking over the lawn to the setting sun coloring the trees outside, I did my thinking.

We'd been here for more than a year. In that time the trees had gone through some changes. From shades of brown to naked—when I saw the sun actually setting behind the Hudson River—to buds. And now the sun's rays came through leaves, coloring them gold.

I had dug showing the sunset to my friend Phyllisia when she had come up from New York the spring before. "Oh, God, Edy," she had said in her singsong West Indian accent. "But this is paradise. I'm so glad for you and your sisters."

It was a nice house. Mother Peters had bought it with the insurance money from her husband's death ten years before. A large white frame house, it stood on a small hill—not far from the railroad station but far enough not to be bothered by the trains. A lot of land spread around it, and a long driveway led up to the front of the house. Across the street was a tree-grown lot, which we used for our picnic grounds.

Phyllisia *had* been happy for us. But I remembered how years ago she used to brag about her apartment in Harlem, back when I used to live in that broken-down railroad flat, with drunks and addicts hanging around our building thicker than the trees in the lot across the way from Mother Peters'. It blew my mind knowing that this house was nicer than Phyllisia's, and the streets of Peekskill cleaner than those of our cold Harlem neighborhood.

Which didn't stop me from missing Harlem. Missing Phyllisia. I wanted to run after the train when she left and go back with her to those streets where we had walked and talked and had become best friends. For a long time after, I had itched to break out, leave the house and family. Keep going. Going.

Watching the suds as they gurgled down the drain, I shook my head. "Naw, I don't want to go nowhere. Want to stay right here with Bessie, Suzy, and Minnie." It had been tough finding and tougher to keep foster parents willing to take in four kids. This was our third foster home in the two years since we had become orphans and had entered The Institution.

Mrs. Brown, the head social worker at The Institution, had really tried. Although she used to say, "Edith, my responsibility, in The Institution, is to get children homes. Keep them moving out. It's simply easier to place one or two children than a family of four."

We had fought. "You promised, Mrs. Brown. And if you can't keep your promise, I can't keep mine. I won't stay. My sisters won't stay. We'll walk. Keep walking."

A straightening fact: she had tried to keep her word. But then with one hundred eighty dollars a head per month, some folks were always willing to take us in, especially when I did the caring for my sisters and seeing that work got done.

Still things always happened.

Mother Gilmore, our first foster mother, had been honest with us. "You kids needs lots of loving, and I needs me lots of money. Got this mortgage to pay, and that's only one thing I got to do in this life. There's plenty others."

Mother Gilmore worked hard. Her house—a brownstone in Brooklyn—had roomers on the two upper floors. She lived on the first floor. In the basement she ran her beauty parlor.

She was pretty, like an actress. Her hair was straightened and hung to her shoulders. She had closets filled with clothes but no time to wear them because of working. At seven in the morning she hit that beauty parlor and didn't get through until twelve at night. Daddy Gilmore too. He worked as a truck driver. He left home at three in the morning and didn't get back until the next day.

Weekends, they partied. Started on Saturday nights. Friends came. They got to drinking and eating and dancing. We girls had a big room with two double beds next to the living room—Bessie and I in one, Suzy and Minnie in the other. When Mother Gilmore had her first couple of drinks, her love opened up. She'd come into our room and wake us up, crying. "Mother's little precious babies," she'd say. "Mother loves her babies so much. She just had to come and kiss them good night."

We got a high off that. We loved her. Dug the glamour, the sweet perfume, the long red fingernails, the long toenails. But then she'd go back to party and drink more. By the time the night ended she and Daddy Gilmore were always fighting.

Most times the Gilmores made up. But I knew some-

18

thing had to happen. Hard work and a little whiskey—good. Hard work and a lot of whiskey—trouble.

One Sunday morning they got to breaking up things—their furniture. When they had finished in the apartment, I heard Mother Gilmore say, "I'm tired. Damn sick and tired of working for nothing."

She went downstairs and started in on her beauty parlor. Daddy Gilmore went to help her. I went to watch them. They never spoke. Just broke up things like they were having kicks. The next morning they were sorry. But like folks say, sorry travels CPT (colored people's time): late. They didn't see where to start putting things together. So they broke up. We went back to The Institution. We had been with the Gilmores for five months.

Fuzzy Mother Pratt was the next one. She had a case of confusion. Seven hundred and twenty dollars every month added to her fuzziness. She lived in Queens and had been the first black in her neighborhood. She was scared of teenagers and scared to death of kids from Harlem. She jumped like a cat whenever I touched her, and so I touched her all the time to see her jump.

Her house was a wreck when we came. We put it together. That confused her more. She'd creep around, searching for things. I'd see her and say, "Hey, you." She'd scuttle off, scared. The kids cracked up.

Mother Pratt always had something figuring. She spent days over her desk with pencil and paper. Then one day I dug that she kept adding and subtracting a budget, or something. I didn't know exactly what she was figuring. But for the hell of it I grabbed her pencil and wrote across the pad, "Seven hundred and twenty dollars." Then I said, "Now ain't no way you can do all that with this money. Just pay your mortgage, lady. Just pay your mortgage."

Mother Pratt skittered out of the room and hid for the rest of the day. The next morning I heard her on the telephone. "Mrs. Brown, you'd better come quick and get them. I'm scared. That Edith is a real toughy." Mother Pratt had had it with us in less than three months.

My sisters got real down every time we went back to The Institution. They hated getting up mornings to the sound of brass hitting brass, of lining up for breakfast at the cafeteria, and of being separated from kids they knew from their old neighborhoods by groups: foster, "troubled," or JDs—juvenile delinquents.

Then there was the business of school. Waiting days, weeks, hanging around the recreation rooms for school records to catch up. And sometimes when they did catch up it was only time to be transferred to another part of the city.

It made me no difference. At The Institution—seeing I wasn't "troubled" or a JD—they let me work in the nursery. I loved working with babies. And there were so many abandoned babies, abused babies, and orphans to care for.

I had my favorites. Mary Allen. She had been two when I first went to The Institution. She had never walked, and I had massaged her legs and got her to walking. Then there was Pip-Squeak. They found him in a garbage can, no bigger than a minute and not much older. He made little sounds: *squeak, squeak, squeak.* I named him, and the name stuck. Yes, I sure loved working in the nursery. It was a lot better than having folks jump away from you scared. Swearing you're tough.

The buzzing doorbell cut through my thinking. I went to let in Uncle Daniels.

FOUR

"Hey there, spring chicken," Uncle Daniels greeted me, laughing his good-natured laugh. He never knew what else to say.

"Mother Peters ain't in yet," I said, just to have something to say. He knew.

I followed him as he walked through the foyer, hung his jacket on the rack at the foot of the stairs, then walked across the foyer to the living room.

We kids never said so, but we didn't like being in the living room except on special occasions or to see special TV programs. It had a high ceiling and bay windows—looking out on the driveway—with fluffy tie-back curtains. The shiny plastic protecting the gold damask material of the couch, two matching chairs, and hassock was too uncomfortable—cold in the winter and sticky every other time. The cellophane wrappings around the lampshades were the same they had been bought in, and we had to be careful not to tear them or to disturb the position of the big colored ash-

21

trays on the tables —although no one in the house smoked. We preferred to fool around in the playroom and feel at home. Yet it always made me feel good to look around the living room and know I helped keep it neat and proper—looking like the window of a furniture store.

Uncle Daniels put the brown paper bag with the candy he brought every night for the kids down on the table. He took out his watch, spent one minute studying and winding it, put it back in his pocket, took his eyeglasses from another, sat down in one of the plastic-covered chairs under the cellophane-wrapped lampshade, opened up his newspaper, and started to read.

Uncle Daniels and Mother Peters believed life and routine were one and the same. He did the same things with the same movements every night. And every night I watched him, ready to call the law or the hospital if he changed one thing. When he had settled, I went on up the stairs.

Halfway up, I heard Bessie. "My father was a great big guy, you know? And we were real rich, you know? He had this big nightclub. . . ."

How in the devil did she stretch her imagination to make our wasted old man into this big handsome dude? She went on like that every night, but the sound of her voice this time brought all my evilness rushing back.

I flew up the stairs and burst into the playroom, shouting, "Okay, okay, you guys, time for bed. And you, Judy, it's time to get on home."

Judy looked at Minnie, surprised that she had to leave so soon. Minnie made her eyes wide to question me. That got me madder. I put my hands on my hips and narrowed my eyes at the little blond girl. Judy got up, but then Kenneth, who had been waiting for Bessie to stop to get his chance to talk, said, "You ain't seen nothing until you seen that ranch my father owned in Arizona. We had hundreds of herds of cows and horses and things. Even wild ones. My dad and I rode every morning. Boy, Dad sure could ride. You ought to have seen him hit that trail. . . ." Then his voice broke. "Oh, God, if only my mother hadn't run off. . . ."

We shifted our eyes away from one another until Bessie charged in. "And you ought to see the long car *we* had. A Cadillac. Wasn't it, Suzy?"

"Did you guys hear me?" I sounded off to stop Suzy, at least, from lying. "Get to your rooms and get ready for bed."

"Who says?" Bobby looked up from his comic book. "It ain't time yet. Mother Peters ain't even home."

True. But that didn't give him reason to challenge me. "*I* said," I said. I chewed hard on my gum, keeping my eyes small. "You want to make something of it?" He stared back, but he didn't have no bones.

"I'm walking Judy to the corner," Minnie said.

"No, you ain't. You get in that bathroom and clean it."

"I asked Suzy to do it."

"I ain't letting her. I told you to do it."

"But, Edy, you know I have to study."

"Too bad. You should have cleaned the shithouse first."

Did I have to embarrass her in front of her friend? I didn't really want to. Yet when she went to walk Judy to the door and Suzy took off behind her, I loud-mouthed Suzy too. "Twins," I sneered. Suzy never looked back.

Kenneth got up, his hands in his pockets, his head lowered. When he walked by, he pulled his shoulders in so as not to have to touch me. Bessie hadn't finished her lying for the night, so she followed him. Kenneth was her best friend.

Bobby sat alone, sulking. Not willing to give me my way, not ready to take me on. "Sho—oot," he finally said. Getting up, he brushed his books to the floor. I stood in the doorway, blocking it. He stared at me for

23

a second, then turned and picked up the books. After he put them back on the table, I let him go on to his room.

Just like that the playroom felt lonely, and I wondered what that scene had been all about. None of the kids had had that coming, not even Bobby. I went out in the hallway to tell them I had been joking. But Bobby had joined Kenneth and Bessie at the door of his bedroom, and I heard them giggling. Right away I thought of Mrs. Bates talking to Mother Peters on Sunday. I got hot and shouted, "Just don't take all night about it, neither."

In the quiet that fell, my ears burned. I whispered to myself, "So I'm flunking out at school. So what, so what, so what?"

"Edith?"

"Yes'm." Mother Peters had come home from her part-time job. I ran downstairs.

"How are the children?" She looked surprised at not seeing them running down behind me.

"They okay." I tried to sound natural. "They just about ready for their candy—any time Uncle Daniels is."

"Ready for bed?" A little frown appeared on her forehead, but I swear that woman had invisible crutches at the corners of her mouth to keep her smile going.

"Yes'm." I went into the kitchen to help her with Uncle Daniels' dinner. She followed.

"So early?"

"Yes'm." I took out the lamb chops, asparagus, and greens for the salad. Special for Uncle Daniels. Uncle Daniels was a natural lamb-chop man. He ate chicken sometimes, fish sometimes. But most days he had his lamb chops.

We kids had had beef stew, which Mother Peters had prepared that morning. Most of the time we had things that I cooked, like hamburgers, meat balls and

24

spaghetti, or ham hocks and greens. We never ever had lamb chops.

As I moved around, I felt Mother Peters' eyes on me and knew that her eyebrows were stretched up behind those gold-rimmed glasses. She didn't go for having her routine upset. I hated being the one who had upset it—for nothing.

I lit the oven, unwrapped Uncle Daniels' dessert: cream puffs. We kids had had Jell-O. I put the cream puffs on a platter, all four of them, then I stood back to admire them. Seemed I never got tired of admiring the cream puffs Mother Peters bought special for Uncle Daniels: crispy light brown, sprinkled with powdered sugar, and real cream inside.

The first time I had ever seen a cream puff had been in Mother Peters' oven, hidden. Where I grew up, around Harlem, there had been no bakeries, and I never had made it much outside of Harlem. So when I saw these things in the oven, I naturally had to try one. I took one bite, felt that whipped cream gushing and spreading inside my mouth, and had to close my eyes. Go—ood. Best thing I ever tasted. That evening Mother Peters said to me, "You know, Edith, your Uncle Daniels likes his cream puffs every evening after dinner. I like to have them for him."

All four? I wanted to ask. Instead I said, "Yes'm." I never questioned Mother Peters.

"Oh, yes'm." All I had done since then was admire the cream puffs—and promise to buy myself some. Still kept promising myself.

"How did the kids do today?" She kept trying to read my mind.

"Okay, okay."

Still not satisfied, she went into the living room. I heard her say, "Dan, the children are ready for their candy."

His big moment had come. He put aside the newspaper and stood up. Blowing out his chest, he took the

25

bag of candy, and with a Santa Claus smile spreading his face out a mile, he went to the foot of the stairs and shouted, "Okay, up there. Your Uncle Daniels is here."

They came tumbling down, shouting just like kids at Christmas. A great bunch. They really liked to please, and it pleased him, that shouting.

Uncle Daniels handed out the candy balls. One to a person. Each took it, thanked him. They were nice kids. They'd die from shock if he ever pulled out something like a Hershey bar.

Mother Peters stood by, studying their faces. "My," she said. "Dressed for bed so early? Whatever in the world happened?"

The kids looked at each other. I stared at Uncle Daniels closing the paper bag. He took it home with him every night. "We just got tired," Kenneth lied. "Decided to get to bed early."

"All of you?" The tight smile. The unblinking eyes.

"Yeah," Bobby said. "We played kinda hard today."

Mother Peters always believed Bobby. "I want to stay here and look at TV with you," he added spitefully.

Bobby had been her companion from the time Mother Peters' husband died until Uncle Daniels took over four years ago. Bobby just hadn't gotten used to being replaced.

"Come on, Bobby, be a good boy." She took the bag from Uncle Daniels and gave Bobby an extra candy ball. The kids looked away. Small things like that got to them. So no matter how evil I jumped, spoiled Bobby remained the main enemy.

On the way upstairs he complained, "Big shit. One extra lousy piece of candy."

"You can have mine too," Kenneth offered, and Bobby snatched it out of his hand and ran. Kenneth took off after him. Bobby made their room first and slammed the door. Kenneth pushed hard against the bedroom door, while I waited, wanting him to open it and grab Bobby. I was hoping that Mother Peters would let them fight. Bobby needed a good whipping. But the minute Kenneth did push in, Bobby started to squeal. "I didn't mean it. I didn't mean it. I didn't mean it."

"Well, say you're sorry," Kenneth demanded.

"I'm sorry," Bobby said.

"Turkey," I said, then went back downstairs.

After Uncle Daniels had finished with his lamb-chop dinner, I set the cream puffs on the coffee table and stood back looking at them. I knew that he knew I never took candy. So just for meanness I stared at the cream puffs on their way to his mouth, wanting to see if he'd open up and offer me one bite one day. But as usual, he kept biting into all that gushiness, his eyes steady away from me.

Then I just stood looking at them. Two middle-aged people, slow-moving, thick around the waist—ready-made for resting. If she wanted to marry him so bad, she ought to ask him straight off. If he said no, move him out. Insurance money didn't last forever. Hell, those cream puffs alone cost a fortune.

"Is something wrong, dear?" She liked to think she read folks' minds. But a straightening fact: I used my eyes as natural drapes around my brains.

"No, Mother Peters. Do y'all need something else?"

"No, dear. That will be all."

Dismissed.

FIVE

"Wednesday."

Whatever whispered in my ear made my eyes pop open. I eased out of bed not to waken Bessie, sound asleep next to me. In the dark I searched for my comb, brush, and bobby pins. They were easy to find. In our bedroom there was nothing fancy to clutter up the dresser. I kept everything in its place and kept after Bessie to make sure they stayed that way. I tiptoed into the bathroom and felt my heart pounding like crazy against my chest as I ran the water for my bath. First slow, but the drippy sound got to me, so I ran it heavy to get it over with. Finally I got into the tub and relaxed. Why had I wakened so early? Had I dreamed? If so, I had forgotten the dream. Then why did my heart beat so fast and my stomach curl so scared?

To stop the answers I got busy scrubbing myself. Next I ran the cold shower to make myself jump, then wiped hard to keep up the tingle. At the sink I scrubbed my teeth and wiped them until they shone. Good teeth—hambone teeth. Never gave me trouble. Then I worked on my smile.

Phyllisia had always told me I had pretty dimples. I turned one cheek, smiled, turned the other. The left dimple went deeper. Had to remember that. But what to wear? Not my blue Sunday suit. He had seen that already. But all my other clothes were plain, ordinary skirts and blouses—he! Who he? And why all this trouble to go to school and come home?

Not wanting answers, I tackled my hair. My hair always gave trouble: too short, no shape, nappy. Even with the relaxer, the back kept sticking out, and the growth next to the scalp stayed hard to comb. But I got to combing and brushing, then brushing and combing. I pinned the sticking ends down with bobby pins, then didn't like the way it looked and took the bobby pins out. Maybe I'd just wear a scarf. . . .

"Edy." Hearing my name unexpected like that, I jumped. Turning, I found Bessie watching me from the toilet seat.

"How long you been there?" Like she'd caught me stealing. 'Whatcha doing up so early any ole how?"

She yawned, her eyes wide and still sleepy. "Edy, why you figger Mama had such good hair and ours turned out so nappy?"

"Say what?"

"Mama. She had such pretty hair, she was so light-skinned—and we all come out brown with this bad hair."

"You crazy or something?" I began thinking of Mama wasting away of TB on her little cot in the kitchen of that railroad flat because the kitchen was the warmest room. Mama's skinny arms were shrunken. Her hair was matted with sweat and so nappy she was too weak to comb it, too weak to do much of anything for herself and less for us. Hearing Bessie trying to make her out like some light-skinned-good-hair woman blew my mind. She sounded as though she wanted to disown Mama.

"You ain't got the sense you was borned with, Bessie."

"How come you always yelling at me, Edy?"

"I ain't yelling. But stop lying about our folks. Mama ain't never had no light skin and Papa ain't never been no strong, handsome dude. Not since we known him. He was nothing but a li'l ole man who shuffled when he walked and walked out on us one day and never got back."

The mussiness in Bessie's eyes kept changing, shifting, moving back. Then only hurt showed. "Get on back to bed," I said. "You ain't got no business being up so early."

Hurting her made me hurt. But our folks were our folks. Talking and saying different didn't make it different. Hell, we were orphans out here in a foster home, and I was working hard to make it ours.

Wednesday mornings Mother Peters made flapjacks and country sausages for breakfast. The smell floated upstairs and always got the kids out of bed, dressed, and down to the table without me having to split my lips. I went down early to set the table.

"Mother Peters." I had to talk about it. "I wish you'd talk to Mrs. Brown about Bessie. She's acting kinda funny. Always making up things—"

"Bessie's all right, Edith." Mother Peters didn't look at me but kept on pouring the batter onto the hot griddle, moving slow like her joints were acting up. "She has her problems. That's the way with kids her age. Make up tales. It helps them help themselves solve their problems."

"Like Bessie!"

"Bessie might need more attention than most kids. But it's nothing for you to worry about."

More attention from a doctor, I wanted to say. But Mother Peters' acting like she knew more than me shut

30

my mouth. She flipped the flapjacks over and looked up.

"You look very nice this morning. I see you're wearing your Sunday suit today. Give Mrs. Bates my regards."

What made her think I was going to Mrs. Bates? Just because I had on my good suit? What was the matter with getting tired of wearing the same old clothes to school?

But I did find myself on Mrs. Bates's street after school, walking past her house. I didn't know how I just happened there. Her street was on a hill the other side of the A.M.E. Zion church. It was at least a mile away from Mother Peters'. I walked by without stopping, just to look it over.

Her house was much smaller—though newer—than Mother Peters'. It didn't have half the amount of lawn space between the houses on either side as ours did, and the walk to the front steps was nothing as long. The gardens on both sides of Mrs. Bates's were surrounded by hedges. I walked on to the corner and remembered I hadn't taken notice of the space in the backyard, so I walked back, going to the opposite corner.

On my third trip past the house I noticed Mrs. Bates's car parked in front of the house with the parking lights on. I crossed the street. A man was stooping, trimming some bushes in the garden. He stood up when I walked up.

"Hey, mister . . ."

He grinned, took off his cap to wipe the sweatband, exposing the baldest head I had ever seen.

"Hey there." He was short, thin. His eyes were warm brown I-can't-tell-a-lie eyes. "You must be Edith," he said. "They're waiting for you inside."

The door to the house stood as open as his smile. I walked up the steps and rang the bell.

"Come in. Come in." A girl as tall as Mrs. Bates but with the eyes of the man outside greeted me as I walked into the small foyer. It had to be Debra, Mrs. Bates's daughter. She held my hands and pulled me into the living room.

"I just came to tell you that—" I began, but I had forgotten what I had come to say.

"Mumsy, Edith's here," Debra called. Mrs. Bates appeared at the sliding door between the living room and kitchen.

"Edith, I'm so glad you made it. I saw that you were angry with me Sunday, and I thought you might not forgive me."

My eyes got heavy from not wanting to look into hers. I stared at her low-heeled pumps.

"I called your house this morning," she said, "but you had already left. I told Mrs. Peters if you came I'd keep you for dinner."

Knowing Mother Peters and her routine, I said, "I gotta go home. I got things to do."

"Nonsense. Mrs. Peters said it's all right. And besides I have a favorite dish I'm preparing."

"And after you've tried it, I'll take you to the drugstore for a hamburger," Debra said, laughing. I laughed with her, liking her. "My mother's cooking is our family's skeleton," she said.

"But Edith will be one of the family." Mrs. Bates smiled through my eyes. "I have adopted her—in my heart. And, Edith when you are a member of this family, you have to take the bad with the good. My cooking comes along with us."

I liked the house. The earth-coffee smell of it. The untidiness—threadbare covers on the couch, an empty cup on the coffee table, a pair of slippers near an easy chair—little things making it look alive.

Then Mrs. Bates said, "Debra, why don't you take

Edith upstairs and talk about the subjects you might be able to help her with?"

Hot blood rushed to my face. I remembered I hated her. I tried to think of something polite, yet sharp, to say. But before I got it together, Debra said, "Mumsy, Edith didn't say she needed help."

"Why do you think she's here?"

"Is that why? I wish someone had told me."

"I *am* telling you, Debra. Edith is having a hard time in school. If she doesn't get help—and right away—she'll flunk out. We don't want that to happen, do we?" Her words were more a command than a question.

"What does it matter what *we* want, Mumsy? Have you asked Edith?"

"I told you, Debra. Edith wants help. She needs help. And who is better qualified to help her than you?" Mrs. Bates's mouth-deep smile underlined the thought: I have spoken.

"What about *my* work?" Debra's brown face darkened. "You know I'm studying for college boards."

"Debra, you have been preparing all your life for those boards. If you have to cram now to pass, it only means you are not ready. At any rate, I know you don't want to deprive your sister of a little of your talent."

Debra and I avoided each other's eyes. "Mrs. Bates," I managed to get out, "I didn't come here—" Why had I come? That certainly was what she had invited me for.

"Don't call me Mrs. Bates." The smile deepened. "That's too formal. Call me Mumsy or Moms. Moms I like better. I never could make Debra call me Moms."

Sometimes in life there is only one thing to do and that's laugh. I did. "Mrs. Bates." I laughed. "It don't make no difference to me if I flunk out. Why should it make a difference to you?"

"Ooooh?" She drew it out, let a silence settle around

33

it to make me think over what I had said. I did. Started to say it over again, but Mr. Bates came in.

"Mrs. Bates," he said, "do you know you left the lights on in the car again? Let me have the keys."

She reached back for her pocketbook on the couch and smiled. "And you can call Mr. Bates Pops," she said. "But only when you're ready. You'd like that, Mr. Bates?"

He gave a twist-of-lemon smile. "Do I have anything to say about it, Mrs. Bates?"

"Of course you do." She gave him the keys.

"I do? Okay, EdithyoucanbeamemberofmyfamilyandIamsayingitquicklytomakesurethatIamnotleftoutofworldshakingdecisions."

His face had a love-folks quality anyhow. And it was so funny the way he ran his words together that I forgot I was angry and grinned. Mrs. Bates said, "Edith, you have the loveliest dimples." Just like that I wanted more than anything to please her.

And so I found myself upstairs, with Debra eyeing me across her desk.

"That woman." Debra was so angry she shook. "She'd drive an angel to take speed. Anything to get away from her."

"But you still here."

"Never mind. I keep planning to leave," she answered. "I really keep planning." She pouted, tapped her foot. Then: "Well, what do we do? Do we talk over your work or do you sit around while I get to mine?"

I looked down at my Sunday suit, fingered the collar of my acetate blouse. There was no denying who I had dressed up for now. And he wasn't here.

"Who all is coming for dinner?" I asked.

Her eyebrows shot up into a question mark. "What's that got to do with math, history, or a cup of tea?"

"Is Browny coming?"

"Browny?"

"I mean your cousin."

"What cousin?"

"Your mother's nephew. The one in church with her Sunday?"

"James? Who knows?" Then she laughed. "James lit out of here so fast Sunday he looked like Lucifer on his way to hell. Talk about a scared somebody. He really thought Mumsy had decided to save his soul."

"That mean he ain't ever coming back?"

"Not coming back? He might be here tonight, tomorrow, and then he might not be here for six months. One thing is sure, he's bound to show up sometime." Talking had rubbed out some of her anger. Now she looked at me real patient. "Okay, what are we going to do, Edith? Do we talk about your work or do I get to mine?"

It made no sense, my taking up her time. I had been planning on quitting school—if I didn't flunk out—for so long that just the thought of going through the term was like a hard-labor sentence.

Still, if I cut out my chances for coming around, I might cut out my chances for ever seeing James. It was sure that Mrs. Bates had not been able to pull Debra or Mr. Bates into church Sundays, and from the way it looked to me, she'd never pull James in there again. And like I had admitted to myself that I had dressed to see him, I had to admit to another straightening fact: I sure wanted to see him again.

I hunched my shoulders. "We can talk about mine to start. Then you can just go on with your own work. I'll hang around."

SIX

I did hang around. The last weeks of April turned warm. The days were getting long, and every evening after dinner I went over to Debra's. Mother Peters didn't dig that break in her routine, but she had to encourage my learning. I left it to Suzy to take over helping her with Uncle Daniels' dinner. Yet every evening when I came home and Mother Peters asked, "How did it go, dear?" I saw that strain pulling at her smile.

Pretending with Debra was a bore. She'd mark places in books for me to read. Then when she finished her work, we'd go over mine. But James just didn't come. Then one day I thought of the reason right in the middle of a page.

"Is he married?"

It took Debra a few seconds to look up from her work, her eyes wide, round, serious. She wanted to be helpful. She looked at the book I was holding, then up at me. "What? I didn't hear the question."

"Is he married?"

"Who?"

"James."

"No, he's not."

"What does he do?"

"I don't know," she said, impatiently. "All I know is he's Mumsy's nephew, my dead Aunt Margaret's son. He lives with my other aunt in New York. Is there anything else? Oh, yes. He's thirty-two and too old for you."

Thirty-two! He didn't look twenty-two.

She looked at me with her see-through-you honest eyes. I looked away. Guilty. We really dug each other, but we were not on the same pulley. Debra was really into learning. I knew it and I tried to stay in the background.

"Edith," she said, "I really don't mind helping you. But I have so much of my own work, and I—I don't feel you are really interested."

I looked into my book, tried to make sense of the words that were now jumbled together. "Maybe we ought to give it up," I said.

Saying it relieved me. I didn't want to take up her time. Especially since James didn't seem to be coming back. And I actually missed being home with the kids.

"I'm sorry I wasted your time," I said, getting up.

"Edith, don't feel that way. It's just that—that—" That I had wasted her time. Only I had known it from the first, and it had taken her a little while to find it out.

"I'm really sorry," she said. "Because sometimes you come on strong. Then I think I'm doing you some good. But most of the time, Edith, I get the feeling that—that—" That I don't give a damn. True.

Whatever Mrs. Bates said, Debra's and my roads led to different places. Mine to the factory, to a job to make it possible to take care of the kids instead of letting them be shifted around. Debra's led to college and whatever she wanted. Why kid ourselves?

I walked to the door, anxious to get back to things that I knew, now that we had both made up our minds.

"Edith—why don't you come around on Saturday? We can go out together—the movies or something?"

"Cool, Debra." That made it better. I liked Debra, and I didn't want to lose her friendship. Weekends made it better all the way around—anyway, it made more sense that folks living in New York visited the country on weekends.

Downstairs in the living room I found Reverend Jenkins talking to Mrs. Bates. "Leaving already, Edith?" Mrs. Bates asked. She looked at her watch.

"Yes'm."

Reverend Jenkins stood up when he saw me. "This is the Jackson girl, isn't it?"

I edged toward the door. "See you, Mrs. Bates."

"Edith . . ." he called, smiling. "Isn't it?"

"Yes, this is my girl, Edith." Mrs. Bates smiled at me. "How are your daughters, Reverend?"

"My daughter Mary Ann will be—"

"I mean your foster daughters."

"Oh. Well, quite well."

"The quiet one—what is her name?"

"Elizabeth?"

"Yes. I tried so hard to befriend her, but she's so quiet."

"But a lovely child, Mrs. Bates. A lovely child. Unhappily, she will be leaving me soon."

"Oooh?"

"Reaching her majority. Eighteen. I am looking for a place to get her situated. I do well by my girls. Very well." He smiled, his fangs showing.

"I got to go," I said.

"I'm leaving too," he said. "May I give you a ride home?"

"Don't mind walking."

"But it's so far to Mrs. Peters'. And you're going my way." He got to the door before me and stood blocking my way.

"Reverend Jenkins," Mrs. Bates said to him, "I can't tell you how it disturbs me the way you always seem to be fighting me. You opposed me on an integrated center for children, and now on the new wing for the library."

"I don't remember ever opposing you, Mrs. Bates. But it does occur to me that you *are* forever fighting. Why? We are making progress—"

"Progress! Reverend Jenkins, the A.M.E. Zion church in this community was established in 1852. Its members brag about its being the first black church anywhere along the Hudson River. Yet for all the progress this community has made, it might as well have been established yesterday."

"I thought you were doing a remarkable job, Mrs. Bates." His nostrils widened. His hands grabbed at the doorknob, but his voice stayed calm.

"Unfortunately I am not the reverend of one of the leading churches, Reverend Jenkins. And my job, as you call it, might be made much easier if there were more responsible preachers. I think I shall bring *that* matter up before the board."

"That sounds almost like a threat, Mrs. Bates."

"Not quite, Reverend Jenkins. But I think I should make it clear that my fight, as you call it, is always against talk—loud talk that precludes progress."

He yanked the door open and guided me out to his car. I didn't want to get in. But I did. I had no real reason not to. But as he started the car, I pulled out my gum and got to popping. We rode for a time, along the narrow streets, looking down toward the river, behind which the red ball of sun was sinking. We didn't talk. But just as I thought we might make it home in silence, he said "Tell me about your other sister—the youngest."

"Ellen?" *Pop, pop* went my gum. "What's there to tell?"

"I hear she died of malnutrition. And only four years old. A pity."

"No, suh, she died of measles." *Pop, pop, pop*.

"I understood malnutrition."

"You understood wrong." *Pop, pop, pop*.

"What about your brother—Randy?"

Pop, pop, pop. I started not to answer, but then I said, "He was the oldest. Got shot by a cop for running. Just for running." *Pop, pop, pop*.

That really got me hot: folks digging into my family's lives. What did he care about them? And why did The Institution put my business in the street? All somebody like Reverend Jenkins had to do was ask, and they all of a sudden got loose bowels in their mouths. I stared out the window looking at the tip of the sun. Just before we reached a drop in the hill, I felt his elbow feeling for me. I flattened myself over against the car door, getting away. He stopped the car, turned in the seat, and grabbed my titties. I hit his hands away.

I had had men sit next to me in movies and feel my legs—I had pinched their hands and changed my seat. Men had exposed themselves to me on the streets—I had just looked the other way and kept on moving. But in my mind I always had the plan of kneeing any man who caught me in close quarters.

But in that car I'd have to get on top of him to knee him. No way. "Look here," I began, but he leaned over and opened the door of the car. I jumped out, intending to spit at him. When I turned to see where to run, I found he had let me off at home. I ran up the steps to the front porch. I remembered my spit, but when I looked back the car had gone.

SEVEN

"Well, it's about time." Mother Peters was waiting for me in the foyer. "Where is Bessie? Isn't she with you?"

"With me? No. I been to Mrs. Bates."

"Well, she didn't come home. She hasn't been home from school."

Right away I felt guilty. Like I knew all along something had to happen with me away from home.

In the living room the kids sat bunched together. Scared. What happened to one affected us all. Uncle Daniels kept walking around, stopping to stare out the window. He looked scared, funny, away from his lamb chops and cream puffs. "Esther," he said to Mother Peters when he saw me, "you got to do something now. Guess I better go. You got to call the police."

Funny how sitting over good food had made a weak man look strong. Now he sure looked confused. "I guess I'd better," Mother Peters said, looking at the telephone but not moving. None of us wanted the police. Not just because we didn't want the questions, but because we didn't want to admit that our home might be in danger.

"I guess I'd better call them," she said, still not moving.

"Then I'm going," he said.

Her look said she needed him. Wanted him to stay. Hadn't he eaten enough lamb chops and cream puffs to stand with her and face the police?

I stood at the living-room door watching him get ready to leave. It was like seeing a part of our home breaking down. He put on his jacket, looked at Mother Peters real sad, then walked to the door and opened it. He stood there, thinking in the darkening evening. Then he stepped out on the porch just as two cars turned into the driveway. Bessie stepped out of one of them followed by a white man. Three more white people came out of the other car.

They all came up the steps, and I recognized the man with Bessie as Mr. Arenfeld, the principal of her school.

"Mrs. Peters," he said, "forgive me for keeping Bessie this late. But I'm afraid we have a real problem here." He and Bessie came into the house, followed by a white couple and little girl. They all stood around Bessie. "Mr. and Mrs. Smith's daughter has lost a bracelet," Mr. Arenfeld explained. "A gold bracelet. Bessie has admitted taking it."

"Bessie? Bessie is no thief, Mr. Arenfeld," Mrs. Peters said, a puzzled smile on her face.

"Who am I to say, Mrs. Peters?" Mr. Arenfeld, a tall, handsome man with gray hair and bushy black eyebrows over gray eyes, tried to be cool. "First she claimed to have taken it and given it to a boy. But this boy seems to have disappeared. He has no name and cannot be found. Next she claimed to have taken it and to have brought it here."

"Here?" Mother Peters' eyes blinked behind the gold-rimmed glasses.

"Yes. She says it's here in this house."

I looked at Bessie, noticed a smug look, like she enjoyed being the center of things. She had that mussy look in her eyes. "Bessie is lying," I said. "She didn't take no bracelet."

"Someone took it," Mrs. Smith shouted. "Monica left the house with the bracelet. It's gone. Why are you standing there encouraging her to lie!"

"Look, Mrs. Peters." Mr. Smith broke in. "We really don't want to go to the police. All we want is the bracelet."

"Look, Bessie ." I pushed my face up to hers. "You tell these folks the truth. Tell them you don't know where their old bracelet is."

"My God!" Mr. Arenfeld said. "Don't intimidate her."

Bessie pulled away from me. "Oh, you know so much with your bossy self. Well, let me tell you one thing, you don't know me, see. You sure don't know me."

I stepped back, like she'd hit me. My family had always been close. Understanding. Like I talked, they listened. No one doubted I spoke for their good.

Mother Peters stepped up to Bessie. "Now, Bessie, dear, did you take the bracelet?"

"I did." Bessie looked at me as though she had won a point.

"Where did you put it?"

"In your bedroom."

"Come and show us where it is."

She led us into Mother Peters' bedroom behind the stairs and pointed to the closet. "I hid it up there."

"On the shelf?"

"Yes."

Mother Peters made Kenneth and Bobby take the things down from the shelves. We all searched through them. No bracelet. "Where else might you have hidden it?" Mother Peters asked. I hated hearing her talk to my sister as though she had nutted out. But Bessie just smiled.

"In the drawer."

"Which one?"

"I forget."

All the drawers had to be taken out, searched, and put back. No bracelet.

"When did you put the bracelet in my drawer, Bessie?" Mother Peters said, suddenly remembering. "I stayed home all day today."

"I put it there yesterday."

"Yesterday!" Mr. Arenfeld looked from Bessie to the Smiths to Mother Peters. "But the bracelet has been missing only since this morning. Hasn't it?"

The Smiths nodded.

"Exactly what kind of bracelet did you take, Bessie?" he asked.

"This is a fine time to ask." Mother Peters drew Bessie to her, angry now.

"Gold," Bessie boasted. "It was round and hard with two little balls at the end . . ."

"Monica's bracelet is a chain bracelet." Mrs. Smith loudmouthed like she wanted to take a piece out of Bessie.

"What an ordeal to put a poor child through." Mother Peters looked convinced that Bessie had lied. "Tell us the truth now, Bessie. Did you take that bracelet?"

"No, Mother Peters. I didn't take it."

"Then for God's sake"—Mr. Arenfeld threw up his hands—"why did you say you took it?"

"Bessie likes to make up tales," Mother Peters explained.

"Tales? What rot!" Mrs. Smith cried. "If you ask me, she just made up that tale about the bracelet being round and hard with two little balls at the end to confuse the issue.''

But they left. Bessie kept grinning. The other kids, too, now that Bessie was home and trouble over. I didn't. I kept looking at the mess in Mother Peters' room and knew who I'd get to clean it up the next day. I heard her at the door. " 'Bye, Monica,'' Bessie called. "See you tomorrow." We heard the cars leave. Then we went upstairs to get ready for bed. While we were dressing, the telephone rang.

Mother Peters called up the stairway, "Edith, Bessie. Everything is settled. Mr. Smith just called to say they found Monica's bracelet in her school bag."

EIGHT

It turned me off, the way Mother Peters decided to handle Bessie's "problem." After that night it got so that Bessie stayed downstairs with Mother Peters and Uncle Daniels when the others went up to bed. Right away everything changed in the house.

"Who she think she is?" Bobby got after *me*. His face was all twisted, his mouth poked out. "Seems like ain't no rules for some folks 'round here."

"What you talking about?"

" 'Bout your *sister,* that's what."

"Whoever she thinks she is," I said, "she got to be into something. But *you* got to stay up here and go to bed."

"Yeah?"

"Want to bet?"

No bet. But those narrow staring eyes promised nothing but some trouble. I slammed the door hard. I hated being accused of playing favorites. I never had. Even though I thought that my sister's problems were mine and the rest of the kids' problems rightly belonged to Mother Peters.

Pushing into Minnie and Suzy's room, I found Suzy already in bed. Minnie sat studying at her desk. It took two minutes for her to raise her head. When she did it was only to glance at me. Right away I got mad. It seemed to me that her always studying made her feel she was better than the rest of us. I stared down at her. "You know the kids are doing a burn on account of Mother Peters making a thing over Bessie?" Minnie kept on reading. Finally, she stuck her fingers in her book to mark her place and looked up.

"I suppose that's better than for her to be out pretending she's stealing." Heat spread through me at Minnie's trying-to-be-correct voice. I wanted to hit her. I had been wanting to get at her for a long time. But she stayed just on the other side of pushing me to it. I slammed out of the room. Guilty. I had no right to resent her learning.

Kenneth was on his way to his room when I bumped into him. "What's with Bessie?" he asked. "She getting too good for the likes of us?"

I thought, if you want answers, get to the back of the line, white boy. Aloud I said, "Go ask Uncle Daniels."

Waiting for Bessie to come upstairs, I got to thinking it just wasn't right for me to stand back and just let things like that happen. So I went down to the living room. There they were, a little family, looking at TV. Bessie, already in her nightgown—one that made her big titties look like a size forty—was curled up in Uncle Daniels' lap, eating a cream puff!

That smile had to have been nailed like a cross to Mother Peters' mouth: someone eating Uncle Daniels' cream puffs and she still holding on to it.

"Bessie, you come on upstairs," I said.

"Edith, leave Bessie be." Mother Peters got up and pulled me out of the room. "You know Bessie's got problems," she whispered in the foyer. "Let me handle her. How are the others doing?"

I tried to look through her eyes, but the gold glint of rims stopped me. I went back upstairs.

In the sewing room at school the next day, I heard a sound: *cluck*. Saw my hand had joined the sewing machine. What had I been doing? Threading a needle? Changing the bobbin? Just thinking? The needle speared through my thumbnail, the foot held my thumb down. It wiped my mind blank.

All around the room girls were busy sewing. Machines going *swosh, swosh*. Teacher bending over, helping someone. There I sat, not moving. It didn't hurt. No pain. Why holler? I tried moving the wheel: stuck. Tried to lift the foot: stuck. I laughed. "Teacher," I called. She didn't hear.

I imagined myself sitting like that all day, joined to that machine. Songs came: my machine and me; married to my machine; on this day I mechanically wed. Might make some long bread.

"Help. Help." The room got quiet. Everybody looking. Nobody seeing. "Help." I kept grinning. The teacher walked over. Got excited. Almost got me excited. Commotion. The mechanic came.

He tried to lift the foot, turn the wheel. Nothing happened. He had to take the machine apart. Then, the needle still in my thumb, he rushed me to the hospital. The thumb still didn't hurt.

The doctor X-rayed the thumb after the needle was out. "There's a steel chip at the bone," he said. "We'll freeze the thumb, cut off some nail. You game?"

"Sure. It don't hurt."

They froze the thumb, cut off the whole nail. Pulled out the chip, then scraped and scraped to make sure no steel was left. X-rayed again, then bandaged me from finger to wrist, put my hand in a sling, and sent me home. "Best get some rest," the doctor said. "It's more of a shock than you think."

Go home? Nobody home. Miss Crip herself and no one to show. I dawdled along the streets. Didn't even know where my feet were heading until they were climbing the steps to Mrs. Bates's door. I rang the bell and stood cradling my hand on my chest like a baby as she opened the door. Then I stood waiting for the concern to show in her eyes.

"Ooooh?" she said as her eyes left my serious face to settle on my bandaged hand.

"Only my thumb." I grinned. "Needle broke off in it."

"How?"

"Sewing a straight seam." We laughed.

"You must have a lot on your mind," she said as we settled down in the living room.

"Sure do." Then, for no reason that I know, I got to telling her about Bessie and Mother Peters and Kenneth and Bobby. Told her how the boys resented Bessie's special treatment. I didn't talk about Minnie. Didn't want to tell her about my jumping mad at Minnie. I had no good reason and didn't want to hear the reason she'd give.

I ended with, "Don't make no sense her carrying on over Bessie and getting the others jealous. Sure Bessie needs attention. All the kids needs attention."

"And so you broke a needle in your finger."

"Not for attention."

"Of course not." I didn't dig the way she said that, so I decided not to hear.

"I just wish she wouldn't, that's all."

"Who?"

"Mother Peters."

"But Bessie does need special attention—from what you tell me."

"Not that way."

"Mrs. Peters is only trying. People do what they know, Edith."

"But she's wrong."

"How do *you know*?"

"I know more about kids than she do. I know my sisters."

"But you're only seventeen."

"Eighteen—in a few months—November."

"Then you'll only be eighteen."

I wanted to laugh again. But she didn't—she kept looking at me, her eyes blackness without the sun. And because they didn't shine I kept looking. Didn't like their message. Decided to go, but they held me. Her messages had nothing to do with me, what I happened to be about. Yet my feet had led me here. I had not been sent for. I had come.

She crossed her legs, fingered her pearls. "I don't mean that you are too young to know. Or that you are wrong, Edith. It just doesn't matter if you are right."

"Then what matters?"

"That Mrs. Peters, wrong or right, makes decisions on what she thinks is right and makes mistakes accordingly—about Bessie, your sisters, you. Edith, you don't count."

"But I will. Soon's I'm eighteen and I get a job I will."

Mrs. Bates shook her head, kept on shaking it. Like a damn magician, she fixed her black eyes on mine. "You will never count. Not unless you decide to break the rules, take hold of your life, and make yourself count."

"I don't dig where you coming from, Mrs. Bates."

"I am saying, Edith, that *you* will not be able to go to The Institution and tell them, 'I am eighteen, a factory worker. I am ready to take over the care of my sisters.' "

"Mrs. Brown said—"

50

"Mrs. Brown lied. Or perhaps I should say—misrepresented the facts."

I hated her. Yet I sat listening, answering.

"Mrs. Bates, I swore on the grave of my ma, on my sister Ellen's soul, I'd take care of my family!"

"Sentiments," she snorted. "What about you?"

"Ma'am?"

"Who is to look after you?"

"I look after myself," I said. "I been looking after myself."

"You are seventeen. Is your life over?"

"Over? No way. I'm gonna take care of my sisters."

"And I am saying you cannot do it. Oh, you can get a job. Buy food. Maybe even see that they have a dress, shoes, now and then. But can you guarantee them they will walk with their heads at the right angle? Live in pride? You, so young. What great accomplishments in your life have prepared you? The Institution can't do it, and they spend millions. Parents can't, and they spend their lifetimes. How dare you think yourself capable?"

"I'm Edith Jackson!" I talked loud, wanted to scream, the veins in my neck stretched from holding back my screaming. But her eyes lit now, kept daring me. "I quit school and worked when my old man walked out. I scrubbed floors, did all kinds of work in white folks' kitchen. All the kids had was me. Me! Edith Jackson! I raised them!"

"Yet no one is proud of Edith Jackson. No one will ever be proud of Edith Jackson. No one will ever be proud that Edith Jackson did her duty and looked after her sisters and did a good job."

I cradled my hand to my chest, wanting to bring her attention back to me. I had no feeling in that hand and that was the worst feeling of all. I had come for pity, I had to admit. But I had come to a woman who had no pity. I rocked my arm in the sling, sorry for my own self.

51

"But they are not grown yet, Edith. They had to go to The Institution." I kept quiet, searching for words, trying not to think of baby Ellen, about the doctor saying she had died of malnutrition.

"They will grow, Edith, get big." Mrs. Bates kept on. "But raising them? What guarantees that any family of four will march to the same rhythm? Particularly when the one doing the raising hasn't developed a tune?

"It's a matter of choice, Edith. One has to have choices. You cannot plan a life on raising your sisters simply because you have no choice. Nor can they think of living stuck to you because they had no choice.

"Too many of our young people are pushed into all sorts of situations—crime, drugs, you name it—because they have no choice. And the matter of choice has to start here." She pushed her finger against my forehead like she wanted to drill a hole. "You have to know, in there, that there are other things you can do. Find them."

"Look, I got a choice," I said, ready to jump to my feet and take off. "I can walk away."

"And do what?" Her quick comeback held me, made me want to protect her from me.

I heard myself say, "Get a job. Look out for myself."

She looked at the sling around my neck, let her eyes follow it to my hand against my chest, resting dead, lifeless, a cold thing between us. "Sewing in a factory?" she asked.

"What's wrong with that?"

She laughed, dry, serious. "Edith, do you know that the first free school for blacks was started back in 1789 in New York? Yet today we either compete for the lowest-paid jobs or are products of The Institution—in one way or another, our minds institutionalized, getting pushed here and there, an inner nation of causes, that blacks, liberals, intellectuals fight over.

"Whatever the reason, Edith Jackson, that's why, unhappily, we save our pride for those who push against those doors—forever barred to us—and make it. Make it into the system—writers, lawyers, teachers, doctors, actors, politicians. They count.

"Edith, have you ever given any thought to the professions? Medicine? Law? Nursing . . ."

I laughed. "You crazy? Me?" I kept laughing, relieved she had gotten back to something I didn't mind dealing with. "Them folks ain't training me for nothing like that."

"You see?" The gold pushed through the black in her eyes, pinning me to the sofa. "You have no choice, have you?" Trapped by words again, I wiggled, uncomfortable. "In this poverty situation, orphans—the abandoned ones—are by far the most vulnerable."

"Ma'am?"

"Vulnerable—meaning they can most easily be used; they melt more easily into that mass of numbers called statistics—faceless statistics. And nothing is worse than being one of the faceless."

A pain stabbed me under my arm. I jumped up. "Lady, you said it all! Why me! Why you mess with me instead of one a them who got faces!" I backed toward the door. Hurt. Mad.

She smiled. "I thought you'd never ask," she said, getting up too. "I thought you'd never get around to knowing why I captured you. That's what I did, you know?"

So she had led me by the neck, like a cow, to ask her what she wanted me to ask. "Because you thought I dug you the way I was looking at you all the time." I put my free hand to my hip, tapped my feet, staring her in the eyes.

"No. Because I said to myself, there goes an orphan. Seventeen—looks like seventy sometimes. An orphan to her soul—like me. Like my baby sister, Mary—but more like my older sister, Margaret."

53

"You an orphan?" My anger burned out at the thought of this retired lawyer being an orphan.

"Yes." She kept smiling. "One never gets over being an orphan—when it happens young. Just being out there, alone, becomes the force that moves your life—for better or worse. That's why, Edith, we orphans always find each other between earth and sky out there in the world."

I smiled up at her, liking the sound of that. "Yes," she said. "Margaret, Martha, and Mary, three of us. But Margaret didn't grow like we did. She was like you, the oldest. Smart, but not knowing it. Smarter than me—I'm sure of it. But she never knew. She never felt she had a choice—except to look after us.

"Edith." Mrs. Bates begged. "You have to know that you are smart. You can read. Your teacher told me. Do you know how many kids today can't read?"

I wished she had stayed away from the book stuff. She had said some hurtful things to me. I wanted to forget them—her being an orphan and all. But I didn't want to be preached to. Whatever she thought, whatever she said, I was Edith Jackson. I had done a lot in my young life, and I didn't want nobody putting me down on account of it. I eased toward the door.

She stood in the little hall, her hands in her jacket pockets, her eyes searching, the full lips riding back over her pretty teeth. She was smiling, yet her dark brown unwrinkled face was dead serious.

"You want to get away, Edith. I'll never keep you if you don't want to stay. But remember, you can keep your hands on your hips, tap your feet, stare the world in the eyes, use every four-letter word invented to defy goodness, chew gum as hard as your jaw will allow, and until *you* decide that you are a person who can make choices and fight for them—you will never begin to count."

I ran from her then. Ran out of her house, down the steps, and kept on going.

NINE

Going home, kicking stones, anything in my way, scuffing up the toes of my shoes. My face burned. *Embarrassed*. My stomach upset. What had made me listen to that jive-ass talk? Me, Edith Jackson, head noisemaker in my own house. Who in the hell was she? "You don't count." Nothing but a retired lawyer talking the crap she might to Debra, maybe somebody like Phyllisia or her sister, Ruby. Not me. I'd been *out there!* I'd taken care of myself. I hadn't waited around for anyone to take care of me. So I didn't have to stand still for her to talk to me like that. I don't count.

Folks supposed to like you for the way you are, anyhow. Not something they want you to be. Witch. Meeting me and acting like she liked me when all she wanted was to try to change me. I nursed my bandaged hand at my chest.

When I got to the house, I saw Bobby in our picnic grounds across the street digging around. I crossed over. "Whatcha doin?"

He glared at me, his face mean. "What's it to you?"

"Just don't be doing something you ain't supposed to. I'm sick." I showed him my bandaged hand.

"Ain't none of your business what I'm doing," he called after me as I went back across the street.

Minnie and Suzy were peeling vegetables in the kitchen, giggling and whispering over a piece of paper they were reading on the table at the same time. When I came in, they stood together, trying to hide it.

"What's happening?"

"Nothing," Suzy answered.

"What you mean nothing? Y'all hiding something back there."

"Really, Edith." Minnie used her trying-to-be-white voice. "You wouldn't understand."

It was as if her voice started the thawing out of my frozen finger. A pain hit me, going right up my hand to my heart. "Why?" I shouted. "Because I'm too dumb?"

"Oh, Edy." Suzy put her arm around me. "It ain't nothing. Why you getting mad?"

I shook her arm off. "Suzy, ain't we alike?" I faced her. "You and me? Ain't we sisters?" She did look more like me than the others. "We plain folks, Suzy. We ain't the smartest. But we count, Suzy. We count."

Her shoulders moved. She was uneasy. Embarrassed, not understanding. "Edy, don't be like that. Reason we ain't telling is because we plan this surprise. You want to know before we ready?" She waited. I stared hard, mad at her for not understanding. "What happened to your hand, Edy?"

I left without answering and went upstairs, holding my wrist tight, trying to cut the pain off. I wanted to lie down.

But Bessie was lying on the bed.

"Why ain't you downstairs helping?" I shouted.

"I don't feel like it." She kept lying there, staring at the ceiling.

The pain in my hand told me to slap her. "I ain't asking what you feel like doing. I'm telling you to go do what you supposed to." She looked at my hand. "Don't pay this hand no mind, baby. Anything I can do with two I sure can do with one."

"Oh, I ain't worried about you hitting me or nothing like that." She put me down. "Uncle Daniels told me that I didn't have to do nothing 'round here I didn't want."

"Uncle Daniels ain't your papa. I'm the one you listen to 'round here, Bessie Jackson. And I'm the one telling you."

I grabbed her by the arm and dragged her off the bed, pushed her to the door. I didn't plan to. The pain made me. Shooting through my hand up to my head, it made me mean.

I kept holding her arm, squeezing. "And while I'm at it, I want you to stop sitting on Uncle Daniels' lap. Stop bothering them old folks."

"I ain't," she shouted. "They want me."

"They just trying to be nice."

She yanked away from me, scrambled to the other side of the bed. "It ain't so. Uncle Daniels want me." Her eyes got real mussy. " I can tell from the way he kiss me."

"Whatcha mean?"

"He kisses me sweet." Her big eyes grew and took up half her face. "He takes candy from his mouth with his tongue and sticks it into my mouth."

I kept looking into those mussy eyes. "Get out of here," I said. I needed more than anything to be alone, to hurt as bad as I was going to. I kept squeezing my wrist.

"Then he rubs my behind and pinches it." She teased. "And he calls me his li'l imp." She let herself fall back on the bed. I went to the door, grabbed the knob, and slammed the door hard. Then I turned and said, "And I guess Mother Peters just sits and lets it all happen."

"That's the fun." Bessie grinned. "Mother Peters be right there and don't even know what's happening."

A line of shooting pain made me shut my eyes. I opened them and saw a wicked grin on her face. "Look, Bessie, I ain't gonna tell you but this once. If I ever see you on that man's lap again, I'm gonna snatch you and damn what Mother Peters say."

Her laughing needled me. Needled the pain.

"See, Edy, you think you know so much. But you don't know nothing. I'm lying and you can't even tell. You sure are dumb."

I grabbed my wrist, kept holding my wrist to cut off the pain. She got up, went out and slammed the door.

I lay on the bed, tried to rest, but pain pulled me up. I walked the room. Walked. Then I went out in the hall.

Bobby, dirty from digging in the woods, pushed by me on the way to the bathroom. I wanted to shout after him to make sure to clean *under* his nails. But I didn't care. I went on into the playroom. Walked. Went back to the hall. Walked. Back to my room. Walked. Back into the playroom.

Suzy came upstairs. "You ready to eat, Edy?" I shook my head no. Kept walking. Later, much later, they all came up, saw me in the playroom, and tiptoed to their rooms. I kept on walking. Pain. Never had pain to remember. Never was sick. And a thumb, a little thumb. One little part of me did me so bad.

Uncle Daniels' car drove up. I didn't go down. Routine, routine, to hell with routine. I hurt. Hurt. Mother Peters came in. She came upstairs. "What happened, Edith?" I shook my head. Kept walking.

Later the kids went down the same as always for their candy. I heard them go. Heard them come back, whispering, complaining, as they went into their rooms. The pain kept on.

Bessie came up, late. She hadn't listened to me. She had stayed down with the old folks like I told her not to. I didn't care. Too much pain to care.

A scream. Loud. High. Jelled my blood. I rushed out of the room. Bessie was running like a wild thing down the stairs, her hair sticking out all over her head, her nightgown flying out behind her. She ran down, screaming. "A snake! A snake!" Crying. Hysterical. Going crazy.

Mother Peters and Uncle Daniels came upstairs, and the rest of us followed them into Bessie's and my bedroom. Sure enough, a long garden snake lay curled up on Bessie's pillow. Bessie stood in the doorway, still shaking, scared out of her simple mind.

"Who did this? Who is responsible?" Mother Peters wanted to know. "Who put that snake on poor Bessie's pillow?" She stared into each face. The kids all looked at each other before returning her stare with a shake of the head. All except Bobby, who kept his eyes dead on hers, never blinking as he shook his head, kept shaking his head, no.

"Edith?"

"Ma'am?"

"Do you know who did this?"

Any fool had to know. "Nope, don't know, Mother Peters."

"You find out who," she commanded me. "Just find out who is responsible, and that person will be severely punished."

"Yes'm." I matched her tight smile, noticed that my hand had stopped hurting—just like that! I looked into Bobby's straight stare, looked back at Mother Peters and dimpled. Deep. Mother Peters did a double-take, stared hard at me, blinking behind those gold-rimmed glasses. Suspicious. Of me? I swear that simple woman made herself believe I'd done it.

TEN

A few nights later, when Suzy and Minnie decided to spring their surprise, Uncle Daniels didn't show. The twins had made a big thing of it, inviting Judy and her mother, Mrs. Cramer. They even made cookies to serve with punch. And it was Mr. Routine himself who held up the works.

"Why we got to wait for him?" Bobby fretted, squirming around on the uncomfortable plastic-covered hassock. He hated to sit in the living room, except when folks didn't want him around. "Maybe he ain't coming," he said.

It meant a lot to Minnie that everyone be there. She sat tense, waiting, her face shining, her bright eyes anxious. "Be patient," Mother Peters said, but her face looked vacant from being worried. She knew that Uncle Daniels never came late.

I stood at the window, waiting for his car, watching some boys playing with a ball in the empty picnic lot across the way. Stripped of their coats by the sudden heat of early May, folks coming home from work walked slowly by. One old woman stopped in front of the window to rest her heavy package and to wipe the sweat from her neck. A man who looked like a wino walked by her in the same direction. He squinted at the window as he passed. Shadows got to resting on shadows, and Uncle Daniels still didn't show.

I stared out the window. I was still mad at Minnie and Suzy for keeping me on the other side of their secret. I didn't care if Uncle Daniels never showed. Why did I have to wait until a stranger like Mrs. Cramer found out something they thought was important? The game on the lot broke up. The boys straggled up the street. The wino must have changed his mind, because he was walking back in the other direction.

"I really don't want to start before Uncle Daniels comes," Minnie said to Mrs. Cramer, who was looking at her watch.

"I'm going on upstairs," Bobby said. I looked back out the window and saw the wino stop and lean against a lamppost away from the house.

The restlessness spread through the room. "Well, maybe—" Minnie got up. Just then Uncle Daniels' car turned into the driveway. I went to let him in.

"Hey, there, spring chicken. Accident on the road held me up. Ha-ha." I saw the wino out in the street, walking past the house.

Uncle Daniels hurried into the living room and sat down. Mrs. Cramer, a small blonde who had thick lips for a white woman, stood up. "Forgive me," she said. "I am responsible for Minnie waiting so long to tell. I wanted this to be a big surprise. You'll all be pleased. Go on, Minnie. Tell them."

Then Mrs. Cramer knew even before me! I stared hard at Minnie as she stood smiling, her black face shiny, her round eyes sparkling. She gave a little curtsy and recited:

"The rain stops movement,
But it brings life.
It imprisons us in our homes,
But it releases flowers, leaves, and grass
To life and to live and to thrive.
So, when you complain about the rain
As it glides and gurgles down the drains,
Just remember we pay a price
For the beauty in our lives."

"Isn't that wonderful?" Mrs. Cramer beamed. We all looked at each other, puzzled. "She won first prize in poetry, your Minnie," Mrs. Cramer explained. "Of all the sixth-graders in the city. Can you imagine? Eleven years old and first prize. My daughter, Judy, twelve—she only won second prize."

"Well, now," Uncle Daniels said, grinning, "we got the two brightest sixth-graders in Peekskill right here in our house tonight. We ought to celebrate."

But Mother Peters didn't take to Mrs. Cramer's being the one to tell her Minnie's news either. She held her smile tight, her dark face blank when she said, "Minnie, I don't understand. Why didn't you say something about entering this contest?"

"She wanted to surprise you." Mrs. Cramer answered for Minnie. She hadn't heard the anger in Mother Peters' voice. "And you were surprised—right?" Mother Peters blinked past Mrs. Cramer. She looked at me.

"And because of that poem," Minnie bragged, "the principal is trying to get me into a special school for bright kids."

"Do tell!" Uncle Daniels, like thick-skinned Mrs. Cramer, hadn't heard of vibes. "Well, can you hold that together? Ha-ha. We got a li'l genius right here in our house."

"Genius, you're right." Mrs. Cramer got up to

leave. "My daughter and Minnie, they're good friends. Almost sisters."

Suzy sat there, looking, listening, and grinning.

At the door Mrs. Cramer looked at Kenneth, kept looking at Kenneth. Then she said to Mother Peters, "You're a good woman, Mrs. Peters. A good woman."

Mother Peters smiled her out, closed the door, looked around at us. "All that white woman wanted was to see the inside of this house. They ain't used to black folks having nothing." Stiff-backed, she walked into the living room, not looking at Minnie.

Minnie, shamefaced now, went upstairs. The other kids went too, except for Bessie, who tried to hang around the living room. But I knew that Mother Peters had private words for Uncle Daniels. I gave Bessie the sign: upstairs. As I stood watching her drag herself up, looking lonelier in that house full of folks than a tree in a graveyard full of bones, the doorbell rang. I went to answer it.

The wino I had seen passing the house stood there. He was wearing a wrinkled but a clean white shirt, and looked as if he had had a recent haircut. The dangers of a safety razor showed in his clean-shaven, nicked-up face. Here was a drunk dried out for a couple of days. "Whatcha want?" I asked.

"To see the laidy." He had an Irish accent, and when he spoke his battered-looking face shook in every muscle.

"What lady?"

"Peters. Mistress Peters."

His knowing her name stopped me from slamming the door, but I shut it tight just the same and went to get her. "A man out there wants you," I told her.

"Who is it?"

I hitched my shoulders.

Mother Peters went to the door, opened it, and right away tried to close it. But the wino had stuck his foot in the door. "What do you want here?" she whispered. "Go away."

He mumbled something and kept pushing against the door. "You know you are not allowed in this house." She kept whispering. "You want me to call the police?"

They struggled with the door, quiet. I just looked. She had almost closed him out when he stuck his hand back in the doorway. "Just a drink of warter, Miss Peters. Just one drink of warter."

"No. Not in this house. You'll not get one drop in this house."

"Please." He pitched his whine high. "One drop like a good laidy. Will you refuse a mahn a drop of warter?"

"Hush."

His whine just went higher. "I ain't asking for much, ma'am. A lousy drink a warter?"

"Then will you promise to go?"

" 'Pon my word, ma'am."

She closed the door. When she turned, she bumped into me. "Edith, go on upstairs with the rest." She hurried into the kitchen.

Me? Dismiss me? When there was a happening? No way.

Mother Peters pushed by me when she came back with the water. She opened the door, but the wino had been waiting. The glass in her hand put her off balance. The wino pushed hard with his shoulder and in no time managed to worm himself inside. He stood with his back against the wall.

"You carn't put me out," he said to her face. "No, yer carn't put me out. I got rights. I got rights." His voice went shrill. He trembled, and sweat ran down his beaten face. "I got a right to be here. You hear? A right, ma'am."

He kept on talking like he intended everyone to hear. And they did. The kids came out on the landing upstairs. Uncle Daniels walked out of the living room, and when he took in what was going on he rushed to help Mother Peters. But she shook her head. She held out the glass of water to Uncle Daniels, but he didn't take it. I could see Uncle Daniels didn't understand what was happening no more than I did.

The wino, one shoulder jammed against the door frame, refused to be moved. "Yer carn't put me out. Let me be. Let me be."

Then he looked up the stairs and called, "Son—son. Help me. Don't let them send me away."

There had to be some sense in that scene. And all at once it came through to me—to us. We all looked at Kenneth. Kenneth, his face pale, his blue eyes staring, walked down the steps, taking them one at a time, like a child learning to walk. Slow. One at a time.

Like bodies made of wax, we stood still as he came down. And in the way of things that seem never to end, he reached bottom.

"Son." The man swallowed. "I—I brought a li'l somethin' for yer." The wino fumbled in his baggy pants pockets and brought out a tiny racing car—the plastic kind bought in candy stores.

The tall, broad, blond, blue-eyed giant of a fourteen-year-old took a few steps toward his father, holding out his hand. It closed around the little car. He held it to his chest. *Funny*. No one laughed.

"Jist a li'l somethin', me lad." The wino tried to smile. "You know? A li'l somethin'—want you to understand—I ain't forgot. Lad—I ain't forgot."

Quiet strained us, drained us. I felt my blood beating in my head. I knew it sort of beat in time with the clock in the living room. The quiet hurt as the boy held on to his little car. Squeezed it so the axle fell off. Then the wheels. The plastic melted into a ball. He kept squeezing.

The father got tired. He looked around, smiling, wanting to bring us into the scene. He had won, his sick smile said. He had come to see his son and he had seen him. No one, but no one, had stopped him. No one had been able to. We were the witnesses.

"That's what I come to tell yer. I ain't forgot yer." The needle had stuck. The dialogue ended. He backed to the door.

"Pop. Pop—"

At the sound the man shrank. Drew into himself. Small. Smaller. Tried to melt out the door. But the door was closed. It didn't open to his fumbling hand.

"Pop—take me with you."

The fumbling hands grew frantic, trying to turn the knob. "I—I—" The wino swallowed, kept swallowing, the skin riding his throat. "Well, yer know, son—the law—"

"I don't care about the law!" Kenneth's voice rose. He was getting hysterical. "I want you! I got to be with you!"

"I—I— Yer know I been looking for us a place. . . ." His mouth quivered. "I—been looking for us a place. . . ."

"I don't care about a place." Kenneth's face grew red; his eyes looked feverish. "I want to be where you are. Wherever you are!"

The little man looked around for help. His eyes shifted fast from one face to the next. His worn smile was shaky now, showing he was doubtful he had won. His searching hands found the knob. He turned it, opened the door. Escape. He had to escape. Trapped. His eyes begged Kenneth to let him go. Let him out. "I—I—I'll send for yer. Soon's I get us a place. Swear . . ."

Licked his lips. Thirsty. But not for the water Mother Peters still held. Real thirsty. He needed a drink for his life. "Ma'am," he said. Respectful. "Yer got maybe—a buck—fifty cents? I—carfare, ma'am . . ."

Uncle Daniels dug in his pocket for a dollar. "Thank

yer. Thank yer kindly." He jerked the door open. Made the front porch.

Kenneth rushed after him. Stopped him. "Pop! Pop!"

He caught the little man on the top step, held him. Kenneth fell to his knees, holding his father, his head buried in the tired, wasted stomach. "Don't leave me. Don't leave me. Take me with you." Kenneth's big body shook, crying. "I'll look after you, Pop. I'll look after you."

Imprisoned by those strong arms, the wino was scared: for his freedom, for his life, which depended more and more on that drink. The wino broke away, stumbled down the stairs, and rushed out into the dark.

"Ple-ee-ease!"

The weird cry released us. We rushed to the door. Peered out. Man and boy had disappeared. We heard running feet, and I ran. Ran in the direction of the footsteps. I knew the way of wine and winos. And I knew the way of boys, the way they got lost forever while running.

I caught up with Kenneth far from home—almost a mile. He was holding on to a wooden picket fence, bashing his head against the pickets. Blood spurted, gushed down his face. His shirt was soaked. His blood had made a puddle on the ground. I stepped into it.

With all my strength I tried to pull him off those pickets. His fingers refused to loosen. I touched his arm and felt steel. That scared me so much that I wanted to run. But I had come to take him home. I worked myself into the space between him and the fence. Crouching, I made myself into a tight ball, pulling together strength. Then I pushed up and hit his chin—hard—with my head. His head snapped back, and I gave him a punch in his throat. He gagged. His hands loosened. I grabbed him around the waist and held him steady as, together, we made it on home.

ELEVEN

I stayed home with Kenneth the next day. I wanted
to. He wanted me to. The bandage on his head covered
ten stitches on his forehead and two on his eyelid. His
good eye kept following me around the room. He hated
me. Hated me for having been there. Hated all of us
for the lying stories *he* had told us. But still he wanted
me—and only me—with him.

I didn't mind him hating me. I had resented him for
so long—for nothing—for being white. Yet his misery
and my misery tied us in that place where prejudice
didn't count. Where nothing counted except understanding: being *out there*. In that, we were sure 'nough
brother and sister.

Sitting next to his bed, my eyes closed, I tried to call
up the face of his father. I might not even recognize
him on the street, side by side with other winos. Small,
weak, faceless. Next to the picture I pulled out the
memory of my old man: small, tired, faceless except

for eyes that had been brown but had faded to watered-down gray.

I got to wondering. What if Bessie—a storyteller like Kenneth—had seen our old man, in this house? On the street? I tried to picture her forgetting her make-believe and running to him, getting on her knees to him, begging him to take her with him.

I shook my head. Remembered the squeaking of his old rocking chair where he had sat rocking, looking out the kitchen window, his back to his roomful of kids. Kids he never spoke to. Love? I never thought of love concerning him. Never thought much of love concerning my mother, either, when she was dying on the kitchen cot of TB. I only thought of my duty.

Ma had had no business having kids after Bessie. Yet she had gone on to have Suzy, then Minnie ten months later. She had dragged her life on for five more years until little Ellen was born.

Lord, to think of that shuffling old man and that sick woman loving and making babies. Making them, then leaving them for me to raise. Duty. Duty from the time I looked up and saw the world. Duty to cuddle, but never be cuddled. Duty to carry, and never be carried. To change diapers, to wash clothes, to clean, to teach. While that old man and sick woman sat around getting sick, sicker, old, older—then dying.

But the old man had done his duty, too. He had pulled his frail body out of that creaky rocker every night and shuffled out of that door to his job on the railroad. Every morning he had shuffled back. We had eaten every day.

We had not cried when he went out and did not come back. Out of habit we listened for his morning shuffle that day. Then we forgot it. The next morning we remembered we had not heard it the day before, and we went on to make plans.

I leaned over Kenneth in that dark room. His eyes stayed closed. I touched his hand. He held mine, tight.

And I saw as clear as anything that my old man was dead.

He had died long ago, that night or that morning. He had gone out that rainy, rainy night and had had no strength to come back. And in Kenneth's mind the faceless man, his father, had gone too, never more to be seen. He had no strength left.

But at least Kenneth had cried. No one had cried for my old man. And ought not a man to be cried over when he had done his duty? When his duty had been all he had had the strength to do? No words, no kisses, just duty.

Leaving Kenneth asleep, I went into my room, threw myself across the bed set to bawl, to cry and cry and cry for a man who had done his duty.

I tried. Strained. Only a lump formed in my throat. I swallowed, swallowed, swallowed. And then I fell asleep.

"Edith. Edith." A hand shook me, Suzy's. "Edith, come downstairs. It's time for dinner." They had let me sleep the whole day.

"How is he?" Mother Peters asked when I came down.

"Sleeping," I answered.

"Good. We mustn't rush him." She whispered as though she was thinking on tiptoe. "It takes time. Poor boy. He has his problems."

Mother Peters had cooked a big meal: baked ham, candied sweet potatoes, greens, and cornbread. Like she'd tried to make up to all of us for what had happened. The food was good, but we all were quiet while we ate, until Bobby snickered and yelled, "Giddup, giddup, giddup, wooooee."

"Shut up!" Suzy narrowed her eyes at him.

"Make me." He smirked.

Reaching across the table, Suzy grabbed him by the

70

collar, dragged him halfway across the table, jabbing her fist to his nose. Blood spurted, greens spilled over the tablecloth, ham thudded to the floor. Bobby wiped his nose, saw his blood. He rushed her, grabbed her around the waist, twisting her to the floor. Suzy rolled him over, sat on him, kept punching him in his face, on his head.

"Give it to him, Suzy! Give it to him!" Minnie yelled.

"Children! Children! What is happening! Stop! Stop, I say!"

I grabbed Suzy. Mother Peters helped Bobby up. "What is happening in this house?" Mother Peters cried.

"He makes me sick." Suzy said. "What about *his* old man? How come Bobby don't talk about *his* old man."

"Maybe he ain't got one." Minnie sneered in her old-time way. "Maybe he *can't* talk about him."

"One thing I betcha," Bobby shouted back. "I ain't ever said my old man was no rancher, no cowboy."

Suzy reached for him again. Mother Peters pushed Bobby behind her. "No, Suzy, he's just a little boy. And it is true, Minnie. He had no father to talk about—either."

Guilty. Our eyes got to slipping and sliding around each other. We knew better. Why blame him for being the first one to come to Mother Peters' house?

We looked around. Looked at the mess we'd made. We all went to getting things in order. Bessie, sitting alone, kept tracing designs on the dirty tablecloth. Staring down, tracing designs on the dirty tablecloth.

TWELVE

For days gloom, like a hand, squeezed that house. Kenneth was getting better, but he still refused to leave his room. Suzy and Minnie tried to make up, but Bobby wasn't letting them. Hurt had fractured his face between his eyes and mouth. It would take time to work that face back into mischief. Mother Peters spent her free time trying. That meant Bessie lost out. Heav—y!

Of all, I guess I was pressed down the most. Someone, somewhere, had unhinged me from me. Nothing that had happened in the house had helped me to get me together. I settled down to evilness, and evil I was the day the phone rang and a woman's voice said, "Edith?"

"Yeah."

"I bought a cake to celebrate Memorial Day. Come on over?"

"Me?" I didn't mind showing my evil mood. "Why me?"

"Because I miss you."

I put the phone down, went outside to where Bobby had been nursing his football. The warm, green-smelling air rushed through me. I pushed him out of the way, kicked the football, and sent it flying over the lawn and through the trees. Then I took off. "Hey, come back and play with me," Bobby shouted.

I kept running. Glad again. Happy again. Young again.

I ran all the way. Up the steps and into the house, through the foyer and into the kitchen.

They sat waiting around an ice-cream cake in the center of the table. "Well, now." Mr. Bates joked. "That didn't take but a couple of hours." He did something with his arms, and I found myself in them, looking down into his Debra-looking eyes, sweat dripping from me down onto his bald head.

"Hiya, Pops," I said, and without looking, I knew Mrs. Bates had smiled.

"I'll mark this day in my book." Pops grinned.

"What happened to you?" Debra asked, her eyes on her father's head.

"I been running."

"I mean why did you stop coming? It's been almost a month."

True. I hadn't been there since the end of April. "Well, I—I—"

"Shall we cut the cake?" Mrs. Bates said, handing me the knife. I took it and stuck it quickly down into the ice-cream cake. I didn't want to talk about my last time here. Seemed she didn't either. But already it had come up. I kept busy cutting the cake, not lifting my eyes to meet hers.

"I thought we were going to hang out on weekends," Debra was saying. "I didn't want you to be mad because of what I said."

"No, no, Debra. I'm not mad at you."

"Well, why—"

"If we don't hurry and eat this cake, we will most

surely have to drink it," Mrs. Bates said, handing me the plates to serve.

I served the cake and we dug in. But a quiet fell that had no business to. I knew it fell because I had nothing to say. Funny. I had run all the way. Why? To sit uncomfortable, not looking at her?

Mrs. Bates didn't like me. She wanted me to be something that I didn't have the mind to be. And I didn't like her because she didn't like me for me. Yet here I sat.

Pops, seeing me embarrassed, leaned over to whisper. "Edith, you can't always take Mrs. Bates seriously. She doesn't always mean what she says."

Not talking about and apologizing were two things different. "But, Mr. Bates"—her eyebrows went up in shock—"I always say things that I mean."

Pops stuck a large spoonful of the cold cake in his mouth and gave all his attention to thawing and swallowing.

Debra stared at her mother. "Moms, what *did* you—"

I cut in this time. "Why do y'all call one another Mrs. Bates and Mr. Bates?"

"To remind folks"—Pops smiled, grateful—"that I count for something around here."

"Not true." Mrs. Bates laughed. "It is because he counts for all things around here. You see, Edith, I had let myself grow quite old when I decided to get married. So old I thought I might never."

"Old?" Pops's eyebrows shot up in his turn. "Is that what you call it? Edith, don't believe a word. That young woman married me to wear me out. Erase me from the scene."

"Old" certainly didn't fit Mrs. Bates. Mother Peters, yes. Uncle Daniels, yes. Even Pops. But not her.

"Look"—she smiled— "Mr. Bates used to file my income tax—for years. And every year I teased him. 'Mr. Bates,' I'd say, 'do you think you'll be around to do my account next year?' You see, he always got money back for me."

"That ought to have been my clue." Mr. Bates nodded. "She'd ask if *I'd* be around. She never doubted that *she* would."

"Then one year he asked me, 'Miss Edwards, why don't you call me Horace?' 'Horace?' I answered. 'By no means. I like Mr. Bates much better.' Rebates, you understand." She winked. "Well, he said to me, 'How does Mrs. Bates sound to you?' Of course I rushed to say, 'I love it. And I accept on condition that you promise to always call me Mrs. Bates.' And so . . ."

"That story has grown gray right along with Mrs. Bates's hair." Debra groaned. But the way Mrs. Bates told the story had changed the heaviness, made me relax.

"Obviously romance is not a prerequisite for intelligence," she said to Debra. "You should try it—it can be a fascinating experience."

"Tell it like it is, Mrs. Bates," Pops smirked.

"Well, here's to shared pleasures." Mrs. Bates toasted him with a spoonful of ice cream.

"Pleasures? Now she tells me." Pops groaned. We laughed.

"You mean you didn't know it, Mr. Bates?"

"Mrs. Bates, haven't you ever wondered why I lost every last strand of my hair?"

"My God, the things I get blamed for." She looked around as though surprised at our laughing. "But then, Mr. Bates, hadn't you ever wondered why I improved so much with age?"

"Often," Mr. Bates said, faking seriousness. "Why do you think I started setting those leg-breaking traps at the back door?"

"Oh, my Lord. Now he tells me. After that fortune I have been spending on my friends in the hospitals."

Funny people. Funny because every time they made a different picture. Never the same. And the hurt she made one time she rubbed out the next—so easy. I laughed so hard my belly hurt.

Then Debra in her straight, honest way touched my hand. "I'm so glad you came, Edith. I felt so guilty about talking to you that way. But I had my work. You understand?"

"Sure, I understood."

"I just hated that you stopped coming. And I got so busy—but I'm all straight now. And if you want me I'll have time to help you out."

"Naw, I don't need no help."

"Ooooh?" Mrs. Bates raised her eyebrows.

"Mumsy, please. You don't know what we're talking about."

"But of course. I know exactly what you're talking about. And you don't need to blame yourself for Edith's not coming around. She didn't come because of me. I told her that she doesn't count and that she never will until and unless she—"

"Mumsy! You didn't!"

"Damn, Martha." Pops pushed his chair back. "I hope you were not that blunt."

"Precisely that blunt."

"Who in the devil do you think you are? The apostle of truth? Who are you to say who counts and who doesn't?"

"I don't, Horace. Society does."

"And what gives you the clairvoyance to tell the future of this or any other society?"

"I had it long before I met you, Horace." Her eyes kept fluid, her smile teasing. "Why do you think I married before I turned forty? To put a body—boy or girl—out here who counted. Who had to count."

"Thanks again," Pops said with his lemon-twist smile.

"Yes, and that's why I insisted on marrying a brilliant man even though he was six years my junior."

"What if you had had a retarded child?" Debra snapped. "You might have, you know? Old women often do."

"But I had you, darling." Her long body relaxed, her smile deepened, the long fingers played with the pearls.

She played with folks! She dug it! It was her thing! Putting words in folks' mouth and having the answer. I saw it. But why had she messed with me?

"Yes, and you have been bending me this way and that, forcing me to think the way you wanted, ever since I was born."

"Is that right? And all the time I thought that your fantastic abilities were due to *your* intelligence."

"But you have never given me credit for my intelligence," Debra shouted. "Picking my subjects and swearing you are only suggesting. Choosing my entertainment, pretending you needed my company. Picking my schools. Well, I'm not going to the college you picked for me, do you hear? I'm not going to Tufts. I've gotten into Brandeis."

"Darling, Mr. Bates will pay regardless of which school you choose. That's why I didn't understand why you tried so hard to keep it a secret. Brandeis is a perf—"

"You knew!" Debra shrieked. The veins stood out on her neck. Her face turned a dark red-brown. "You knew and never said anything. You let me think—"

"Debra, I merely assumed that you did not want to discuss your school with me. That has always been your choice, to discuss or not, love."

"It has not! You are always meddling! You have always meddled! But you can't have it your way. Do you understand? I hate you! Hate you. I'm not staying here much longer. I can't stand it."

"Then you should leave, dear. Mr. Bates will pay

your rent, wherever you decide to live. Won't you, dear?"

"My daughter is not leaving this house." Pops jumped up to stand beside Debra. "Do you hear me, Martha? She will not leave my house. That's what I work for. That's what I'm spending my life for—a home for my child. And she shall not leave! Do you hear?"

"Yes, dear." Mrs. Bates nodded. "You see, Debra, I'm not holding you prisoner here. Your father's love is."

They stood next to me—Pops and Debra—on the same side of the table, and we all were together in our feelings at that moment. Only the two who had the words to answer had no idea that she had set them up. And I, who knew, didn't have the words.

Then Debra looked at me. "You see, Edith, you can't pay that woman any attention. Nothing she says! She just likes to blow off her mouth."

All of a sudden a silence fell as Mrs. Bates rose—all six feet of her splashing a shadow across the table. "Don't you do that to me!" Her face changed to pure street—125th Street at Lenox Avenue, Harlem. "No, baby, never do that to me.

"Blow your natural," she said, deep-voiced. "Get rid of all the crap you been building. But in this house, baby, Mumsy counts."

Debra and Pops melted behind that. It turned me on. She had turned into a woman I knew. "That's right." She sounded ba—ad. "Everybody's body pays Mumsy mind. Just who do you think you are?"

"Sister Margaret's only child." A voice spoke from behind. "The black, black sheep of this fine family, the only boy child, and the love of y'all's life. Now how's that for an entrance?"

James.

There he stood, still in tans and browns, arms outstretched, head back, posing. Pops leveled his anger at the doorway. "Why didn't that black sheep keep his black butt in Harlem?"

"I heard Aunt Martha laying down the law. Telling you like it is, huh, Big Daddy?" He came in, set a paper bag with a bottle of whiskey in it on the table. "But never mind. Look what I gotcha."

"Take *that* with you on your way out." Pops went after his target. "And the next time you come let somebody know. If that isn't too much to ask."

"Mr. Bates, James is our only nephew. He comes so seldom. Let's be nice?" She sat back down, relaxed, her hands fingering her pearls, her lips rolled back into her white smile, and just like that, that woman I knew had slipped away.

James went over and gave her a peck on her head. "Being a pretty man gets 'em every time, huh, Marble Top?" James winked at Pops. Pops walked out. "Hey, Debra." James turned his attention to Debra, grabbing her around her waist. "How about a li'l hug for ole cuz."

"I'm not in the mood, James." Debra removed his hands, glared at her mother. "I'll talk to you later." She walked out.

"Whe—ee," he whistled. "You been raising a li'l hell, ain't you, Auntie? But never mind, Debra," he called after her. "I got me another pretty li'l girl to hug. Whose li'l girl are you?"

He grabbed me out of the chair, whirled me around, hugging me. Then he kissed me and set me on my feet.

The skin from the top of my head to the soles of my feet broke out in happiness—prickling happiness. I knew now why I had come. Knew why, whatever Mrs. Bates said, I had to come again.

THIRTEEN

"Didn't Bessie go out with you?" Mother Peters asked when I got home later. The last time she asked me that jumped in my mind right away. I didn't want to deal with it. I wanted to hold on to that warm feeling, think of those strong arms, that tobacco smell. James.

"I left her here," I answered. "Didn't she go to the picnic with y'all?" I asked Suzy and Minnie.

"No," Suzy answered. "She hadn't planned to. She walked with us to the corner and then she left us."

Memorial Day. She might have gone to another picnic. To the movies. "It's so late," Mother Peters said. It wasn't. Only eight o'clock. But Mother Peters looked strange. I went to ask Kenneth.

"Did Bessie tell you where she might be off to?"

He looked up from his book. "She's not my friend any more. Didn't you know that?"

"She's the closest one to you."

"Before she found her another friend." His lips

curled up. "She ain't been to see me since I—since I fell."

I started to the door, stopped, turned to look at him. He stared at me with his one good eye. He still wore his bandage, and here he was trying to smooth the way for his old lies. But he knew I knew. We all knew.

I thought of going to tell Mother Peters. But I already heard her answer, "Dear Kenneth, he has problems." I went back downstairs to wait with the rest of them.

As usual we waited in the living room. Time rushed by. By ten o'clock Bessie still hadn't come. Mother Peters stood looking out the window. Bobby looked at television. Me too. I stared at the tube and thought of James and his strong arms.

At eleven Suzy said to Mother Peters, "Ain't you gonna call the police?" Mother Peters didn't turn. She just stared out the window. We waited.

After a while I said, "Mother Peters, what are we going to do?"

She turned, looked around the living room. Tired, I thought. There had to be something more for a woman than to go from work to home, from home to work and care for a bunch of children just to keep this big house. Still, her smile held as she walked slow, real slow, to the telephone.

The police came fifteen minutes after she called. There were two of them. One was tall, with light hair and blue eyes; the other was shorter, thicker, with black hair and eyes. The shorter one asked the questions.

"You say her name's Bessie Jackson? What does she look like, ma'am?"

"Brown skin, brown eyes—large. Short hair—"

"Something like this girl?" He pointed to Suzy.

"No—no. Fuller—more developed. Large, large eyes."

"How old?"

"Thirteen."

"What was she wearing?"

"I—I—what did Bessie wear today, Edith?"

"I don't rightly know." Fact was I hadn't thought much of Bessie the whole day.

"She had on her blue print dress," Bobby said.

"Yes"—Minnie remembered—"the one with the red trimming."

"What's new on Bessie?" Kenneth walked into the room. The policemen looked up, then at each other, surprised.

"All these kids yours, ma'am?"

"Yes, my foster children."

"Oh, foster children." Instant boredom. The tone changed to don't-care. "Had any trouble with them before?"

"Trouble? I don't understand what you mean."

"You know. Running away. Fights." He looked at Kenneth's bandaged head. "Trouble with the police. These foster kids can be a damn nuisance." He dismissed the lot of us with a wave of his nightstick. "Always in some kind of trouble."

"Not my children." Mother Peters protested. "Not my children."

Kenneth sat between Minnie and Suzy on the cold sofa. Bobby left his stool to sit next to Kenneth, and I squeezed in next to Bobby. Like we needed the feel of each other to prove our flesh was real, like other folks'. We all sat, staring at the police.

"We'll let you know if we hear anything." The policeman ended his questioning. "Or if you want, you can call. Let us know if you hear anything."

On our way upstairs Minnie said, "That damn Bessie. I sure hope she doesn't fool around to mess up my chances of going to that special school."

"School!" I knew she had to be joking. "You thinking of some damn school when your sister might be out there hurt? Hit by a car? Be in some hospital?

82

Minnie, you might think you better than us. But them policemen ain't seen no difference.''

God, we had always been one closed fist, my family. But it looked like the fingers were just stretching apart.

"Lay off, Minnie, Edy." Suzy put her hand on my arm. "Ain't *you* wondered why Uncle Daniels ain't been around tonight?"

It hit me. Almost knocked me down the steps. They all knew: Kenneth, Suzy and Minnie, Mother Peters, with her slow, tired steps. Hell, I had been so caught up in myself I hadn't even *missed* Uncle Daniels. I ran back down to the living room.

"Mother Peters?" She still stood looking out the window. I hurt for her. She sure had tried. Tried with Uncle Daniels. Tried with Bessie. She sure didn't have this coming. "Mother Peters?"

She turned. Slow. First her body, then her head. Then she was staring at me, her face set, the crutches gone from her mouth, smile wiped out. Had all that hate been hiding behind the cross of that crucified smile?

Did she sure enough hate us? Had she always? My tongue reached back for my gum.

"Mo—Mrs. Peters." Seems I had been forced to say mother once too much. "I—I hope you ain't thinking of calling The Institution tomorrow?"

"Why?"

"Well I wish you'd sorta wait until—"

"What right do you have to ask me to shirk my duties?"

"They might put Bessie in a reform school."

"Why didn't *she* think of that?"

"Well"—I chewed hard—"if you call The Institution, make sure you tell them about Uncle Daniels— the police too. You know Bessie's only thirteen—"

"How dare you? How dare you suggest such a thing!"

All those pretty lamb chops. All that buttered asparagus, mushrooms. All those good, good cream puffs.

"I reckon we both know that where you find Bessie, you'll find Uncle Daniels. If you call The Institution, maybe you ought to tell them that."

"Edith." She stopped me as I started out the room. "I hope you understand that under these circumstances, you and your sisters will have to be returned to The Institution. I did try. But girls have always been too difficult for me to manage. They create —so many problems."

Why answer? Fat-faced liar, liar, liar. What made *you* let Bessie come downstairs dressed in her nightgown? Why did *you* let her sit on his lap eating his cream puffs? How is it *you* never saw when they kissed—sweet kisses? And why, lady, why are you waiting at the window ready to take him in, forgive him, and throw the blame on a thirteen-year-old? Bigassed, fatfaced, two-faced liar. Problems. Problems. Lady, you got them.

BOOK II
The Institution

ONE

"Dear Phyllisia, I'm looking for a new mother again . . ."; "Dear Phyllisia, I hope our next home will be just as nice . . ."; "Phyllisia, Bessie ran off with our foster mother's old man and so . . ."; "Hi, Phyllisia, we are back in New York again. At The Institution again . . ."

I tore up that letter too. Writing letters had never been my stick. And writing to Phyllisia kept getting harder. Time kept passing. It was mid-August, the third month back at The Institution, and I was still tearing up letters. Biting the eraser of my pencil, I looked at Minnie, sitting across the room, reading. Not looking up. Hating to look at me. It had hurt her, coming back. More than it had Suzy. So Minnie just sat in the reading room. It was easier not to talk. I dug that. She had worked hard, studied hard. Good things had been planned for her, had been meant for her.

Hell, what about me? I sat still, waiting for a hot

breeze from outside to cool the sweat on the back of my neck. Hadn't I worked hard too? For her, for them?

I decided to make the letter funny. "Hey, Phyllisia, you remember that home I kept showing off to you—that one I swore I'd work so hard to keep? Well, I'm out again. They shut me out again. . . ."

For some reason Phyllisia's sister Ruby's face flashed across my writing pad. Pretty Ruby, with her brown velvety skin, her big smile, her brown eyes, looking at me, being sorry for me, so sorry. Forcing me to look at that scene where I had met her for the first and only time.

I lay the pencil down and stared hard at it and at the pad. That scrawling pencil had been scratching up old scabs, layer after layer of scabs, getting to a bleeding sore hidden deep.

"We are friends. Best friends," Phyllisia had said. "We will always be. . . ." We were. Even with all her bragging about her fine house, her pretty mother, her rich father and his restaurant, we still had been friends.

She had never cared about my being poor or ragged. Never cared that my shoes were run-over, that there were holes in my socks, that my hair was nappy from my not having time to fix it. She wasn't like her friend Marian, who liked to say for me to hear: "Dig that Edith. Ain't she a mess?" No. Even after my old man had split and I had had to quit school to look after the kids, we stayed friends.

And then that day she brought me home. Her mother was sick, and Phyllisia was afraid of the feel of death. That day the difference between me with my ragged clothes, and her, her family, that apartment with the rugs, the drapes, the lamps all over, showed me the difference between us, as folks. But we were friends.

And though it was true that her mother, pretty in her dressing gown, with her curly hair bunned up on her head, looked different from my mother with her hair matted from sweat, when she lay dying on our kitchen cot—death staring out of dying folks' eyes makes them look the same. Only life matters to folks wrestling with death. And so I tried to bring life to her, though I knew better. But then Phyllisia and I were friends.

I remember Ruby, sitting on the floor, pretty and brown, her eyes begging for praise. She needed praise like other folks need food. I remember her eyes, how glad they looked for me being there, for me praising her. And so I praised her some more—getting rid of that feel of death.

But then *he* came. The father, Calvin. Just thinking of the look of him—standing, big, black, handsome, evil, staring at me, his light brown eyes in his black face—still squeezes my insides together. God! He hated me! Hated the difference between me and his things. Hated my ragged coat on his red sofa. Hated my nappy hair, my run-down shoes on his rug.

"Ragamuffin," he shouted. "Get she out. Get she out." He hadn't looked at me when he talked but at Phyllisia. "Get she out. I don't want no ragamuffin in me house!"

And she turned from me. Turned her back to me. I hadn't understood. *She wanted me out!* She had turned her back to shut me out!

Ruby was hurt and had defended me. Her eyes had turned to sorrow for me. But *my friend* had shut me out!

I walked home. I knew I'd been hurt. I didn't feel a thing. Numb. And with everything happening fast. Her mother—dead; Baby Ellen—dead. The Institution. And every week Phyllisia's letters, letters saying she was sorry. Talking about our friendship. Her being loyal. The one person I had anywhere to hear from. Then:

The Gilmores—shut out; Mrs. Pratt—shut out; Mother Peters—shut out. Pain on pain. Hurt hitting hurt. Scabs the scratching pencil had pulled up. And there, near the bone, that bleeding sore frozen like my thumb had been frozen, thawing like my thumb had thawed. Shooting pains of my life stabbed through me. Still I knew: Phyllisia was my friend.

"Dear Phyllisia, I'm in New York again. At The Institution again. Sure am glad to be near you again . . ."

After searching through my apron pocket, I took out the one piece of mail I had received since my return. "Moms—or Mrs. B—either one. Love," written on a piece of paper folded around a twenty-dollar bill. I slipped the money and note back into the envelope and into my pocket, tore up my unfinished letter, called "See ya," to Minnie, and walked out of the reading room, looking for Suzy.

First I went into the recreation room for foundlings, then I went to the room for juvenile delinquents. I saw Suzy talking to this group—two of them, Dora and Elsie, were from our old Harlem neighborhood.

I knew from their hands and arms, their fast talk, that something was shaking. Dora did a nonstop: "Yeah, I known somethin' went down, see? Yeah. Girl, looked over to her bed, see? I ain't seen her, dig? I say to myself, baby, you had it."

"You mean you know she OD'd?" Linda, the Puerto Rican member of the bunch, asked.

"Well, hell. I knowed she's been shooting, you know? And I knowed she ain't had no home but this. So when she ain't made it back . . . what else?"

"Wow," Elsie, thirteen, said, putting her hands to rest on top of her big stomach. "Things is gonna be happening, you know? We better cool it, you know?"

"Don't make me no difference, see?" Dora chewed gum my style. "Be in court tomorrow, see? And be outa here and on the street."

"If you ain't sent to Hudson."

"Me? Baby, you outa your mind? I'm a juvenile,

90

see? And I only been up two times. Still got one more time before any happenings, see?"

"The Man might fool you. Might pull a switch when you walk in court. Send you flying. Dig what I mean?"

"Shee—it. If I come back here, baby, I'll walk. I know my rights. Know what I mean?"

"I'll walk with you," Elsie offered. "I don't feel like just waiting 'roun' till the Man says when. See where I'm coming from?"

"With that belly?" Dora cracked up, laughing. "Better let the Man keep you right here. That way, you can just hand the kid right over to Edith. Howya doin, Edith baby?"

"Ain't nothing to me." Dora chewed gum as hard as I did and looked a lot tougher, so I double-timed on the gum to show her that I was able to work in the nursery or do anything else I wanted, without her say-so.

"Got to be more to you than's showing, with all that slave you putting down."

"Making time count while I hang around," I said. "And loves that gravy." Meaning that I ate the same food as staff.

"Best you than me, with all them squawking brats. Any old who. Making it out come tomorrow." I didn't pick her up nor lay her down. Dora talked to keep her mouth moving. Wherever the judge decided she'd go. Best proof, she walked out of the shelter every night and came back still talking.

"Hey, Edy," Linda, the Puerto Rican girl, said. "Suzy here tells me that in a couple of months you getting out and getting a factory job?"

"What's it to you?"

"Say she gonna be livin' with ya."

"So?"

"Well, y'all'd be living in Puerto Rico. That's where all them factories gone to. I know. My sister had to move back there to get a job." I hitched up my shoulders. "I ain't lying. I swear to God. I ain't lying."

"Hey, what's with Minnie?" Dora cut her off. "What's she putting down? She acting like we ain't good enough or somethin'."

I kept time chewing, with her, adding a head-to-toe measurement to shake her up. "Ain't nothin' happenin', 'ceptin' she's serious. Dig where I'm coming from?" I said.

"That's cool, baby. Just didn't want to think she'd put us down. You know what I mean?"

"Her natural thing," I said, turning my back to her. "Hey, Suzy, come on, Minnie's needing ya." Suzy walked with me. "Better stick close to Minnie," I said. "Acts like she feeling down."

"Where's she now, Edy?"

"Where else?"

She sighed. We looked at each other, understanding.

"Hear anything on Bessie, Edy?"

"Same zero. Can't find Daniels. Say he moved from where he'd been living for the last twenty years. Got that, Suzy? Seven years before Bessie breathed air, he'd moved there."

I turned to go upstairs.

"You reckon they'll ever find her, Edy?"

"Dunno."

"You think they trying?"

Turned that one over. Thought of our past. Remembered the policemen at Mother Peters'. "For folks like us? Shee—it."

Four-year-old Mary Allen ran up to grab my skirt when I went into the nursery, and together we walked down to the other end—ducking screams, holding away from outstretched little hands, looking away from tears running down cheeks to mix with snot, then with dribble from slobbering, crying mouths, shut my ears not to hear the shrieks. Kids naturally knew how to shriek needle pricks into the gut. It made it hard to pass them up. But I did.

Sooner or later those who cried for attention got it. But Institution kids, kids like Pip-Squeak, had never known a home with a friendly hand or body. Didn't know how to cry for it, or got tired early from trying with no one to answer. And so they lay quiet as rag dolls in their cribs.

"Squeak, squeak, Pip-Squeak," I said, bending over him. "'Cause if you don't it's sure you'll lay in that shit for the rest of your days."

I took off his diaper and got to scrubbing the dried crust from his backsides, scrubbed hard to get him clean. He never whimpered. When I first got back, he had had open sores on his backsides, but keeping him plastered with A and D ointment had cleared them up. Massaging the bald spot at the back of his head had brought out a bit of fuzz, and massaging and exercising his legs had strengthened them to the point where he actually stood up.

"Them that demands attention's the ones that get it. Don't you know that, boy?"

His eyes brightened on my face, but he never smiled and didn't squeak. Two years old now, and no squeaks.

"Mary Allen, go to Mrs. Ortiz and say, 'Please, Mrs. Ortiz, Edy wants a diaper.' "

Mary Allen let go of my skirt and ran behind the attendant, Mrs. Ortiz. I waited, looking at her running, thinking how I had worked on her legs until she had walked. She had been two when I first entered The Institution. Now, at four, she still didn't talk.

"What did I say to ask for?" I called to her. She took her thumb out of her mouth, looked at the stout Puerto Rican attendant, busy changing another child's diaper; then she stuck her finger back into her mouth.

"I said to say . . ."

Mrs. Ortiz handed her a diaper from the stack on

the wagon. Mary Allen ran back to me. "Thank you," I said. "Now you say to me, 'Edy, you are welcome.' " Mary Allen stared hard at my mouth, sucking her thumb and pulling at her hair with her other hand.

"Thank you. Thank you. Please. Please. Edy. Edy." I kept repeating words as I massaged Pip-Squeak's legs, pulling and pulling and working them like a bicycle. I stood him on his feet, put my finger in his hand, and pulled. Anxious. He stiffened. I put his hands on the sides of the crib and left him standing. No bigger than a minute. No weight to carry. He had to walk. Had to.

I went to the next Institution baby. "Now, Mary Allen, go back to Mrs. Ortiz. Say to her, 'Please, Mrs. Ortiz, Edy wants a diaper. Please.' Please."

Mary Allen took her thumb out of her mouth, stared at my mouth, put her thumb back, took it out again. "Pees," she said, then ran down to Mrs. Ortiz, laughing.

"Hey, come on back. You get a hug and kiss for that." She ran back to me. I picked her up, hugging her. I walked over to Mrs. Ortiz. "Mrs. Ortiz, Mrs. Ortiz, Mary Allen just said please."

"Oh? That nice." The short, fat woman smiled. Not believing.

"Honest," I said. "She's so cute. I don't know why someone ain't adopted her."

"People," she answered, "no like retard—"

"That's a lie. She ain't retarded," I said, getting mad. "All she needs is someone to care."

"Why you look at me?" She got hysterical. "I got but two hands. I no slave."

I hadn't meant her. One nurse and a few underpaid attendants had no way of taking good care of all the abandoned, abused, and orphaned children sent to The Institution. But just the fact that they hadn't sent Mary Allen or Pip-Squeak to one of the Catholic or Jewish agencies for foundlings frightened me. Once they pinned the tag "retarded" on a kid, it went to one of the retarded homes.

"Look," I begged. "I ain't talking about you. But you got to know that Mary Allen is smart. She's smart as she can be. I can prove it."

"Prove it," she said. "You eighteen soon. Come back be attendant like me. Prove."

I flashed heat. Looked past her to Mrs. Bristol, the black nurse standing reading charts at the other end of the room in her white starched uniform, with the black band around her white nurse's cap, looking professional. "Woman," I snapped, "just give me one of them diapers." I snatched it from her hand and walked away, mad.

TWO

"Edith Jackson. Edith Jackson. Wanted in Mrs. Brown's office. Minnie Jackson. Minnie Jackson. . . ."

Don't know why the sound of my name and Minnie's over the loudspeaker made my heart skid and slap across the insides of my chest. But going toward the office it did.

I got there first and so had first chance to look into Mrs. Brown's professional smile. "Sit down, Edith. I have good news for you and Minnie."

Now, if there was news for me and Minnie, leaving out Suzy, from the jump that had to be bad. And I knew it when Mrs. Brown picked up that steel letter opener, held it at both ends, and flipped it over from one side to the other as she sat back in her seat, her "sweet and kind" face blank except for that smile.

Folks used smiles like tools. They used them to grab and hold you. To punish you, to fool you. Mrs. Brown, with her tan skin, her reddish-brown hair, her eyes a blend of the two colors, used her smile to blind you.

"I hope," she began the minute Minnie walked in, "that both of you think the news as good as I think it is." Her gaze slid off my face so I expected not to. "Let me first say that this has been in the process of happening since you first came back. I thought it better for all concerned that it be finalized before I told you, Edith."

Why me? I glanced at Minnie. Her round face, her eyes, everything shining. She already knew! A chill worked up into my stomach.

"Everything is settled now." She spoke directly to Minnie, and my sister's smile changed to a glow. "We have a home for Minnie. It gives me great pleasure to tell you this. I have every reason to believe it will be permanent. I'm sure there is a real possibility of adoption."

Fingers played the flute with my heart. "What about Suzy?" I asked.

"This is a chance for Minnie, Edith."

"We a family, Miss Brown. You . . ."

"I know. And I promised to do all in my power to try to keep you together. I tried. As you know, Edith, it hasn't been easy. But I did try. You have been with The Institution for less than three years, and in that time you have been in three different homes. I don't have to tell you that if there had only been one or two of you it might have made the difference of being permanent.

"Our responsibility, Edith, lies in doing what we think best for each ward. I must say again that I *am* pleased to have had this special request for Minnie."

"Minnie is only eleven, Miss Brown. We—me and Suzy—is all she got as family. How can it be best—"

"We weigh these questions carefully, Edith. It is because Minnie is so young that we think it is in her interest to be a part of a stable family situation. Suzy too. And I am sure that we will be getting her a home soon."

"Miss Brown, Suzy and Minnie's like twins. How you gonna part them?"

"We have been forced to take Minnie's remarkable intelligence into consideration. We like to think that we encourage growth and development in our young charges. And when Dr. and Mrs. Cramer requested—"

"Mrs. Cramer!"

"Yes. They have gone through a great deal of trouble to—"

"But she's white!"

"And Jewish," Mrs. Brown added. "We are not a racist institution, Edith, and while we do give consideration to ethnic and religious backgrounds, there are times when other considerations transcend these—"

"Like when?"

"Like when both child and parent have the need, express a desire, to be together. Minnie, I must warn you that it will not be easy—"

"I don't care," Minnie burst out. "I'll work hard. I'll study. I'll be smart!"

"Ain't they groups fighting against—"

"Yes, black groups are fighting against interracial adoption. Interreligion?" She shrugged. "Edith, your first foster mother was a Methodist. Your second foster mother a Catholic. Mrs. Peters an A.M.E. Zion. Black children, you see, just don't have the luxury of choices. There are so many of us."

"Minnie." I turned to my baby sister. "Tell her you won't go. Tell her you won't leave Suzy." *But she had said she wanted to. They had already discussed it. Behind my back. Even behind Suzy's back!*

Minnie stared at the floor. At the wall. Then she leveled her eyes into mine. "I'm going, Edy. I want to go. I want to more than anything. You hear? More than anything."

Minnie had never looked anything like Bessie. Her small round eyes were nothing like Bessie's big stary eyes. But right then I got the feeling of Bessie staring

98

at me, saying, *"You don't know me. You don't know nothing."*

I looked at Mrs. Brown. She kept flipping that letter opener, back and forth, back and forth, back and forth.

I went into the waiting room to talk to Mrs. Cramer when they came for Minnie the next day. Saw Dr. Cramer for the first time. They both looked like moving picture folks. She, small with blond hair, full lips. He, tall, thin, handsome.

"Mrs. Cramer," I said to her, "Minnie and Suzy ain't never been apart."

"Tut-tut," she clucked. "I know. What a pity."

"How come you can't take Suzy too? They just like twins."

"But then you'll be alone."

I hate people who try to put me on. "It don't matter about me. In a li'l while I'll be eighteen. But they—they got a long time."

"What can I say?" Mrs. Cramer shook her head. Sad. "Minnie's got a good mind. Do you want her to waste it? And you know—we're not rich."

"Minnie and Suzy can always sleep together."

"Minnie, she'll share Judy's room. They're already like sisters. Where is the room—"

"If there ain't room for one, oughtn't to be room for neither." I didn't intend to let them off easy.

"But why are you mad at me?" she asked. "Look, a girl like Minnie, what's she doing in a place like this?"

And what am I doing here? And Suzy? And Mary Allen? And Pip-Squeak? Not fair. *What did I expect from her?*

"Suzy's a good worker." I changed my tone. "She can do most things. She can clean good. Wash dishes. Scrub floors—"

"What are you saying?" Dr. Cramer cut in. "Are

you saying that your sister must be our maid? I'm not sure what you mean.''

Sin and crime are different. I had committed a crime against my sister. Guilty. Guilty. Guilty. Tongue-tied, ashamed, I looked away when Suzy came in with Minnie. But I felt her through me, my plain-looking sister. Plain like me, without my dimples. Not smart. Just an orphan looking for a home. And what did that have to do with a twelve-year-old maid?

Suzy had been Minnie's shadow for so long, yet she accepted Minnie's going. She had tears in her eyes, but she accepted. Shadows don't fight when their substance takes leave.

I went over to Suzy, put an arm around her, holding her tight. Letting her know that she still had me.

We stood, Suzy and me, watching from the window as Minnie got into the car. We waited as the car pulled away from the curb, and we stood staring at empty space after the car had gone. What to say? What to say?

"We just like those damn little Indians, Suzy. Now ain't but two of us.''

THREE

They found Bessie.

A car skidded off slippery Riverside Drive one rainy night and took a dive into the Hudson River. They fished them out—Bessie and her Uncle Daniels. Suzy and I went to identify the body. This young Puerto Rican official went with us to the morgue. No Mrs. Brown. No Mrs. Peters. Just Suzy, me, and this young dude we had never seen before.

At the morgue the official left us looking through this glass partition at something lying on a hard rock bed. He went behind the glass and pulled back the sheet. Suzy screamed. Screamed and ran. Why had they sent her? This twelve-year-old? The official took off after her. I chewed gum. Hard.

I suppose, like Suzy, I had figured it to be a mistake. No mistake. Bessie lay there, hard and cold and lonely. She sure had hated being alone. Alone, on that concrete bed, her mouth drawn back over her teeth, her nose pointy, skin gray from being in the water—or just from being dead.

Randy had looked ashy. Black and mad and ashy. But Bessie lay as gray as a mouse. A lonely dead mouse. Funny, I hadn't noticed how pointy her face was, how small her hands, how thin her little arms. Always had seen those wide, mussy eyes, the big titties. Eyes closed now. Titties big, hard—a big-tittied mouse.

I kept chewing. It kept me from cussing. Suzy's bawling hit my ears, kept messing with my throat. I swallowed at that lump. Kept swallowing. It reminded me of the day I wanted to bawl over the old man but had fallen asleep instead.

I had cried for Randy, though. Looked through this same glass partition and had cried. Had cried when little Ellen died, too. Guess I used up all my tears. So I chewed and swallowed, swallowed at those lumps.

Bessie Jackson, Bessie Jackson, you are dead. Dead as you will ever be. You ain't no more. Did I love you? I sure gave you enough hell. And you hurt me. Looked dead in my eyes like that and saying I didn't know you. You hurt me, little girl. But I sure didn't know you. Didn't know you, little old girl. You hear Suzy crying? Did she love you? Did anybody love you—enough? Did Uncle Daniels?

Kept looking at her titties, wanting to see them go up and down, up and down, fool the life back into her body. But she just lay on that cold, hard bed, dried out and lonely. A dead mouse.

The official touched my arm. Time to go. I turned. Stared at him, feeling old. "You know," I said to him, "my ma had six kids. Six. Ain't but two left." I wanted to take that back quick—say three. Remembered the look in Minnie's eyes and repeated, "Two —two."

All the way back Suzy cried. I let her. I didn't want her crying. Our lives had been too hard. I didn't want her wetting my shoulders with those heavy, heavy tears.

Back at The Institution, I made a quick change, wanting to get to where being kept busy kept folk from thinking. But no sooner had I slipped into my apron when the loudspeaker voice called, "Edith Jackson. Edith Jackson. Wanted in Mrs. Brown's office."

I took the well-chewed gum out of my mouth, threw it away, armed myself with three new sticks, then went for my face-to-face in the office.

"Edith." The face-wiping smile. "I'm sorry not to have been with you today. I—"

"Sure. Sure. Busy." I just waved my hand. "I didn't need nobody with me to tell me that thing laying there had been my sister."

"Edith. Let's not be hard on each other."

"That what you wanted? You sorry? Okay."

"I did want to tell you that I'm sorry. But I also wanted to tell you that we have a place for you. Special request. . ."

"And Suzy?"

Mrs. Brown shook her head.

"No way." I worked on my gum. Did she think we were pieces of blocks to be shoved about on a patchwork shuffleboard? "Miss Brown," I said to her, "we just got back from the morgue. Bessie's lying there. Dead. I know to you it's one a them things—part of the job. An accident one day. An overdose the next. A fight. A stabbing. There goes another one."

It hit me. How many of us came through this crap—life? Compared to other folks. Of my old lady's kids weren't but two to go.

"Suzy is taking it mighty hard, Miss Brown. She ain't but twelve. Now you saying I got to split. Abandon her. . ."

"Don't make it sound that way. I know it seems—"

"You don't know nothing, Miss Brown. You sure

don't know a thing if you think I'm gonna walk out on my sister. I don't rightly dig where you coming from. We may be bl—'' Funny talking to tan-skinned professionals. They called themselves black—our hitting-back name—so it didn't make sense in saying black. Instead I said, ''We may be poor but we still people.''

''I know it sounds heartless, Edith. But these foster parents are—''

''I ain't going!'' I stared hard at the bookshelves over her head, letting my hard-working jaws nail down my message.

''Be eighteen in a few months. And I'd just as soon serve out that time in the nursery. Don't try getting me no home. I ain't for wanting to make foster folks' life better—and I quit expecting them to make mine. Know what I mean? If you try to push any more fosters on me, I'll just start walking.''

''Why, Edith? You'll only be caught. Brought back. Or worse. Maybe sent to a reform school.''

''Who you kidding? I'm seventeen. I ain't committed no crime. You'll just write me off as an emancipated minor, that's all. If you got time to waste, waste it on them JDs that legs it outa here when they get ready.''

She threw down the letter opener, put her smile away, and stood up. ''I guess this is not the best time to talk to you. You are upset. Understandably so. Let's talk later in the week. But I had hoped the idea of going back to Peekskill—''

I had slammed the door hard behind me when the name Peekskill came jamming up against my head. Peekskill? I put my hand in my pocket and grabbed the letter. My breathing caught, hurting in my chest. Peekskill?

My breath eased out, I turned to go back into the office, but another girl pushed by me going in. I walked away. Went halfway up the stairs. Stopped. Sat down, staring at the door of the office.

''Edy, I been looking for you.''

Suzy came from upstairs and sat next to me on the cold marble step. I didn't look at her. Guilty. Always guilty where Suzy's concerned. Resentful. What made her any different from Bessie? From Minnie? In a year, a month, even tomorrow, she'd be telling me off—"Edy, you don't know me."

"Edy." Suzy's heavy-with-tears voice confused me. "Why did it have to happen to Bessie? Oh, God, Edy, she ain't hurt nobody." Wetting my shoulder again. I kept staring at that door to the office. "Sure, she was simple. But being simple ain't no sin."

"Simple? She always been simple, Suzy?"

"Long's I can remember. But that ain't no reason for her to die like that."

Made no sense. Bessie simple? Always? I tried to remember those shut eyes open, the mussy look. Guess I'd been too busy looking after the kids ever to really see them good. I wanted to see Suzy now. See through her eyes into her head. But I didn't want to look at her face. I kept staring at that door.

"What's gonna happen, Edy? What's gonna happen to us?"

Death forces folks to think. Scares them. It sure had scared the hell outa Suzy. Death had always been around us, but Suzy'd never had to face right up to it like today. Showed her her own loneliness. What to say? I shrugged.

"You and me, Suzy? Most likely we'll get old. Then we gonna die too." Hold out a promise. Hit her with the truth.

And sitting on those steps, looking down at the cold marble leading to Mrs. Brown's office, we two plain orphan girls faced the truth and it calmed us. And feeling her calm, I nudged Suzy with my elbow, smiled, winked. She managed a weak smile herself. Then we went our ways.

FOUR

Bessie's big-as-life face hung right over my head when I got into bed. Gray, mousy eyes staring—dead eyes. Dead and mussy. I tried to move out from under, squinched down in bed to get away. But Randy stood at the foot of my bed, grinning. "What's happening? What's happening?" I shouted but heard no sound. "What the hell is happening?"

Ruby's head suddenly hung down over my bed, her sad eyes dripping hot tears, burning me. I didn't know Ruby was dead. "What did you die of, girl? What you die of?"

Shuffling feet, the knocking of a cane sounded in my ears, and Papa came walking out of the wall! "Papa!" I shouted my silent shout. "Where you get that cane? You ain't never had a cane to get back home. You simple—you simple—you simple—" Like a needle getting stuck in a deep groove, my mind kept spinning around, while two pools like melted tar that the sun had sunk beneath moved up to me from the window.

So I didn't stop Papa from climbing on the bed and walking onto my head, with that cane knocking, knocking. I kept looking at those pools while trying to shake him off, but he walked down my face, knocking, knocking. The cane slipped into my open eye. Digging into my open eye. "Papa, don't mess with my head now. You messing up my mind." He kept on walking down my face, his feet light like nothing, but the cane poking, poking. The pools of blackness hanging over my head held my gaze so I didn't see Papa when he walked down my chest, poking at my heart. I shook my heavy-as-lead body to get him off. He kept on going. The black eyes with the sunken sun kept holding mine. Papa's cane dug into my body, pushed hard into my womb, hurting so that the blackness of the eyes melted into the sun and the sun burned right through my eyes. Then I heard this voice calling: "Ed—ith. Ed—ith." Like an echo in an empty cave. "Ed—ith. Eeed—ith." James! "Whatcha want?" I shouted my silent shout. I tried to move my legs to run—run to James. If I reached him I'd be safe. But my legs didn't move. James kept calling. "Eeed—ith." Then the sun fell. It raced down toward my head. I jumped out of bed. No. I found myself sitting up in bed, my night-gown soaked with cold sweat and me shivering, shivering. It was morning.

The nightmare faded. Only one part remained: the sound of James calling me.

Phyllisia and I used to talk about telepathy. Of calling someone you cared for and needed and of them hearing no matter where. James had called me. He sure sounded lonely. Looking out of the window, I breathed deep of the cool-earth September morning and knew what I had to do. "Just because I promised we'd die," I said to myself, "don't mean we got to die *together*." But how to tell Suzy? What to tell her?

She came and sat on my bed while I was still dressing. "Edy, Dora didn't get back from court yesterday. Maybe they sent her to Hudson!"

"God, Suzy. Sure am sorry."

Not true. It took some guilt off me: coaching from Dora Suzy did not need. And it had nothing to do with her being picked up for shoplifting. Before The Institution I had gone for slick. Being poor made being slick important.

What did you do when you had forty cents, needed a package of gum, and had to pay forty cents over the counter for a loaf of bread? You kept the chewing habit for free. If you had fifty cents for a subway ride and your stomach had gone to growling, it meant that the hot-dog man got the change, the city paid for the subway ride. When you had ragged drawers and the sixty-cent pair had just been hiked to seventy cents, you kept your sixty cents for spending and you still had your dignity. Ain't no dignity in having to wear ragged drawers.

No, Dora had other things going for her, knew strange scenes that twelve-year-old Suzy didn't need, especially when I wasn't going to be around to protect her. But it made the telling harder so I pushed it back for later.

But a timer inside me had got to ticking. Kept my feet moving. And when I dressed Mary Allen, she got the beat. She knew and held tight to my skirt as I marched between the yelling and shouting and the outstretched hands to get to Pip-Squeak's crib. I smacked his butt instead of smiling into his brightening eyes. "Yell, you simple mother's child. Shout!" I said to him. "Tell everybody out there that somebody mothered you. Scream your lungs out, boy. Don't just lie there."

From the shine in his eyes, the kicking of his legs, I knew he thought I'd praised him. "Li'l boy, if I had lain in shit as long as you, I'd be on my feet raising a real stink."

I set him on the floor. "Now walk. You hear me? I want you to walk." I let go of his hands. He stood there wavering. Mary Allen let go of my skirt. She ran, grabbed his hands, and pulled. He fell.

"Let him be, Mary Allen. You worry about talking. I'll worry about him walking." That hurt her. She stuck her thumb in her mouth .

"Now you two-year-old mother's child, I said walk, and I want you to walk and I ain't fooling." I stood him up. "Walk."

"Edith, don't push him so hard." Mrs. Bristol stood over us. "He's made real progress since you've been back. You should be proud. But don't push him so."

Progress? Progress for a two-year-old to walk? "He's two years old and he ain't retarded," I said.

"What do you mean by that?"

I held my tongue, thinking, you heard. You been letting him lie in shit for two years. Why hold him back now?

"I mean—that he ain't retarded."

"Who are you to say what he is or isn't?" She stared me down. Didn't like my attitude. I looked down at her white shoes. I knew the signals: We might not have enough hands, too many babies. But if you get an "attitude," baby, I'll restrict you. Bar you from these quarters.

No time to be smart. No time to be sassy. Sure, you need me more than I need to be here, but I ain't here for long. I took low. "I just thought—" I grinned. Remembered my dimples. Made them deep. "Some folks might think he's retarded. And you and I know he ain't." Kept grinning.

She stared. Weighing. No, she still didn't like my attitude. But I had taken low. An extra hand still made more sense than restrictions. She walked away.

"Now," I said, grim-faced, serious, when she left the room. "You listen, Pip-Squeak. You gonna walk, you hear me?" He stared at my face, felt my beat, held tight to my fingers, setting his mind to it. His mouth pinched. Feeling for balance. Unblinking. His eyes on my face. Feeling for balance.

Something happened in that room: cries, screaming, yelling, everything stopped. The nursery shrank from silence. Legs came around us. Children's legs, gray uniformed legs, white, starched uniformed legs. I never looked up. Kept all my attention on Pip-Squeak. He kept his on me.

I fought for my fingers. He held on. I fought for my fingers. He held on. Determined, I fought for my fingers. An old man's sigh shook his little body. He gave them up. I held them inches away. His eyes stayed on my face. He reached out. Not far enough. He took one step. Wavered. Tried to gain his balance. Tried to move his other foot. Fell. A sound of spattered flesh, the pulp of over-ripe fruit. I pulled him up. Round eyes, dry, gripped mine. He held on to my fingers. Let go. Gained balance. Took one step. Wavered. The other foot. Balanced. His eyes left my face. Found my hands. One step, the other two, three, he ran, fell into my outstretched arms.

Cheers. Applause. Screaming, crying, shrieking all went up at the same time. I held him. Swallowed at that lump and held him. "Pip wak. Pip wak. Pip wak."

Over and over the words passed through my ears. "Pip wak. Pip wak."

A loud laugh. "Oye. You hear. She talk. She talk."

Mary Allen hitting me. Little hands pounding my back. "Pip wak. Pip wak."

I reached behind. Grabbed her. Held them both to me. Close. Close. Swallowed that simple lump. "Mrs. Ortiz." I looked up at the smiling woman. "These kids ain't retarded. Neither one of them's retarded. I swear they ain't."

"Retard? No. No retard." She smiled. Kept smiling.

I tucked them into their cribs that afternoon. Happy. Sad. I knew I'd never see them again. I put a finger

110

in Pip-Squeak's palm. His hands tightened around it in his sleep. I walked down to Mary Allen's crib. Kissed her. She sat up. "I'm going away," I said. "And this time I'm not coming back." She sucked hard on her thumb. Reached up and grabbed her hair with her other hand. She had known. But then she hadn't expected me to stay. For her no one ever stayed. I walked to the door, feeling her tears, yet knew she'd never shed them. That four-year-old had learned to live.

FIVE

Leaving the nursery, I took the wad of gum out of my mouth, threw it in a basket, went to the office, knocked, went in.

"Edith, I'm glad you came." She grabbed the letter opener, reared back in her chair, gave me the professional.

What now? A change of mind? Of heart? It made me no difference. My days at The Institution had ended.

"Edith, I—we have been most fortunate. We have found a foster home for Suzy. She left this morning."

"This morning?" I had to pick up my pieces and stick them together before I spoke. "But I talked to her this morning."

"Late. After you had gone to the nursery."

Why had she made it easy? "Without telling me?"

"I didn't want it that way, Edith. Believe me. But you have been most uncooperative lately."

But not this time, lady. This time cooperation had

been the name of the game. Why didn't you see? Why didn't you let me tell her? Let me deal with me?

"Edith." *She* looked guilty. "You have no idea what a great responsibility we have here, trying to get homes for all these young people. It is not easy, Edith. We have so many people to answer to—"

"Why didn't you let her say good-bye?"

"Believe me, it's better this way. I didn't want to run the risk of another scene. It has just been too difficult."

"Where did you send her?"

"Brooklyn. A very responsible family."

But weren't they all responsible families?

"Under the circumstances, I think it best to withhold her address until you—until you both are adjusted to your new situations —"

"When will I be leaving for Peekskill?"

Without looking, I saw the smile relax her body. No, lady, no more fights from me. This time you picked a winner.

"First thing in the morning," she said. I turned to leave. "I am so glad that you decided to go. I know you'll be happy. And so will Reverend Jenkins when he hears that everything is settled."

I stopped my hand on the doorknob. Then without once looking back I opened the door and walked out.

BOOK III
Choices

ONE

I heard a bell ringing and woke to a straightening fact: I had pushed the button. I looked around, saw the hedges enclosing the short walk, saw the chrysanthemums, shouting bright yellow in the dead garden. Looked out into the clear September evening just as a wind blew through my coat on its way to scrambling leaves off the trees.

I shivered. I was scared. How had I come all this way without one thought? One plan? No, I had a plan. I had intended to leave The Institution and make it up to Phyllisia's. Yet I had gone to the train station, bought a ticket, ridden the train for over one hour, and here I stood. A hidden plan? Why? I waited for an answer in the footsteps of the person opening the door.

"Edith!"

Surprised? Natural. What about the face? What feelings there? A raised eyebrow? A polite smile? No way to tell. The light spilling through the door, putting me on the spot, left the face in the shadow. I listened to the silence. That seemed to go on and on.

"Don't just stand there," she said. "Come on in."

But the silence had been too long. I held tight to my suitcase, turned to leave. "What in the world— Girl, come on in here." She reached out, took my arm in one hand, my suitcase in the other, pulled me into the house.

The smell of the house hit me. The warmth of the house reached around to hold me. I wanted to take off my coat, run up the stairs, down again, play at being home.

"Mr. Bates," she said, "will you look at who walked in this door? Do you call it coincidence or miracle?"

Pops. Sitting in his chair, reading the newspaper, his feet on the hassock, the light reflecting off his bald head. The months faded. Had I really been at The Institution? Had Mary Allen talked? Had Pip-Squeak walked?

"Whichever one," he said, "doesn't matter. Where did you come from? Come give the old man a kiss." I went to him and he put his arm around my waist, drew me down to him. Kissed me. She hadn't kissed me. She never had kissed me. I had never seen her kiss anyone.

"We were just talking about you," he said. "Just then when the bell rang. We hadn't heard from you. Mrs. Bates said she had written—"

"In my fashion," she said. "I had hoped you'd answer."

"I—I ran away," I said. "They were going to place me with Reverend Jenkins."

"Oooooh?"

"I walked away—this evening."

"But isn't it strange—about Reverend Jenkins? He must know you'll soon be eighteen—November, isn't it?"

"I didn't know where . . . I came to . . ."

"I'm glad you came. Welcome. I thought of you—kept thinking of you."

That was cool. Like she had put the whammy on me—long distance. Brought me back.

"Sit down, sit down." Pops pulled me down on the hassock. "Mrs. Bates can never conceive folks do get tired."

"Or hungry," she added. "What about some food?" Without waiting for an answer she went into the kitchen.

"You look good, Edith," Pops said. "They treated you well?"

"Okay. They might overlook some of us"—I laughed—"but they don't *try* to mistreat us."

"It's good that you came. Debra's away at college. The house seems so empty. I hope you can stay with us for a while."

"But of course Edith's staying," Mrs. Bates called from the kitchen. "Where else will she go? She can spend the night in Debra's room, but I'll fix this room down here so she can have a room of her own."

"What about Reverend Jenkins?" Pops asked.

"What about him?" She stood at the sliding door.

"He can be nasty."

"Ooooh—he has a monopoly?"

"That he hasn't, Mrs. Bates." Pops shook his head. "But he has the law—on his side."

"The law? To have Edith for a few months, he'll use the law?"

"A possibility."

"At any rate we have Edith—possession is nine points. Edith, your dinner is ready."

Sitting in the kitchen, eating dried-out chops and tasteless peas, I kept listening. "Reverend Jenkins is not exactly happy with you trying to get rid of him as pastor, Martha. And he might just be delighted to get something on you—like a criminal charge—harboring a runaway?"

"Mr. Bates, I never expected to go through life without once going against the law. Did you?"

"To be frank, I hadn't thought much about it."

"Then it's time you did. If Reverend Jenkins really *wants* to make trouble, both you and I might be classified criminals." She teased. Pops sounded serious.

I got up. "Look, you folks are great. But I didn't come to stay. I got to go. I just come to—"

"Because you wanted to."

She walked up and down, up and down the living room, while Pops still kept trying to read. "I wouldn't worry about what Pops is worried about," she said. "All you have to do is stay near the house and don't answer the door while we're out."

"Martha!" Pops threw down his newspaper. "Do you expect Edith to stay in this house as a prisoner?"

"Only until we see what he has on his mind."

"And what about Edith? What has she to say?"

"About what, Mr. Bates?"

"About what she wants. Haven't you noticed? She hasn't said two words—no, that's wrong. She did say, 'I got to go.' "

"Don't be funny, Horace. This is really serious."

"Isn't that why you ought to ask Edith just what she wants?"

"But we know what she wants."

"And that is?"

"To be here. With us. She came, didn't she? All the way from New York City to Peekskill? To be here. And here is where she will stay until we decide what she ought to do—particularly about her studies."

"We?"

"Horace, of course we cannot do anything without Edith. Stop being a fool." Her voice toughened. But then she laughed. "Anyway, Mr. Bates, you know as well as I that young people don't always know what they want. We are here to give directions. You know? Directions?"

She kept up this walking and thinking. Pops looked at her for a few minutes, then turned to me. "Edith. Stay. I want you to. But only if *you* want. I don't care about Reverend Jenkins. And I am not really concerned about the law. I'm sure our lawyer here can handle both. What I want to be sure of is that you make your own decisions about your own future."

"Mr. Bates." The smile. The charm. Fingers playing with pearls. "Sometimes I do suspect you of being really very ordinary."

"And what's wrong with that?"

"Nothing. Nothing at all. Most people are, you know. Without even trying."

The next morning, in her bathrobe, without pearls, elbows on the table, big person-to-person smile, she tried for chumminess. Didn't make it. It hit me quick that her mind kept sifting. Setting up *my* answers to a talk *she* wanted to have. So I kept my eyes on my eggs, trying to head her off. I had heard her at it. Didn't know how to deal with it.

"These are some boss eggs," I said.

She sipped black coffee, smiled. "I do make excellent scrambled eggs. That's why my family puts up with the rest of my cooking."

"Eggs sure are good."

Sipped her coffee. Kept looking at me. And me? Scatching through my mind to keep her off me. "What you think will happen with Reverend Jenkins?" I asked.

"Reverend Jenkins!"

Scored. Her mind had been other places.

"I—do have some questions—about Elizabeth. Do you remember Elizabeth, his foster daughter?"

I nodded.

"She reached her majority. She's gone. I keep thinking. She is sort of your type—small, wiry, strong. I have to find her. There are things I must know. . . ."

Our thinking had met. I had never talked to anyone about my ride home with Reverend Jenkins. Had hardly thought about him since. But when Mrs. Brown had sprung his name, everything had clicked. Streetwise.

Mrs. Bates smiled at my understanding. She sipped coffee. "Reverend Jenkins has been blocking progress in this community. His supposed concern is sin." She laughed. "Methinks it's time for a new reverend. Elizabeth might just be the way. . . ."

I stared at my plate. She wanted me talking. A slip of a word. I ate the eggs, slowly. She sipped coffee. The last of the eggs finished. Didn't want to lick the plate. I got up. Stacked the dishes.

"What are you doing?"

"Gonna wash dishes."

"Not in my house." She laughed. "Don't you know I don't allow anyone to wash dishes in my house?"

Not true. I had washed dishes here. Washed and wiped, helping Debra. And she had seen me. Did she want a dispute? Careful. I felt for words, not wanting to give her her head. "What you want me to do 'round here?"

"I hadn't been aware I advertised for help."

"I got to do something."

"Are you saying I keep a dirty house?"

I kept my head still and tried not to look at the disorder in the kitchen. Keeping house had never been her thing—one reason I had liked the house.

"No'm." The quick smile made me think that "no" might have been the trigger, so I added, "But I just can't sit around doing nothing."

"But you have so much to do already."

The trap was sprung.

"Look." She got up, threw open the door to the

122

little room off the kitchen. I walked into the neatest room in the house. It had been her junk room. "I got up early this morning and cleared out your room. I wanted to surprise you."

Surprised? It stunned me. The bed had been made, and on the desk was a neat pile of books. Pens, pencils, pads. Everything neatly arranged.

"Of course, I don't expect you to just sit around. That wouldn't be fair to you—or to me.

"When I knew you had flunked out at school, I kept wondering how to get you back, get you here, get you interested in a program. In my day, in New York, we had night schools. It was hard work going to school nights and working days. Only the most ambitious ever made it.

"Thank God, today there is the High School Equivalency—then there are the college programs around New York. While you're studying you can be making up your mind on just what you intend to do—to be."

She lifted my chin, smiled into my eyes, her eyes trying to see through to the back of my mind. "You made me very pleased when you walked through that door, Edith. And as long as I can, I will back you—all the way."

"Mrs. Bates." I picked my words. It wasn't easy, telling someone trying to be nice that what they wanted and what you wanted was different. Book learning was not my thing. I didn't dig sitting in a room, door closed, my mind deep in torture. "I sure appreciate you wanting to help and all like that. But I just want to stay on here till I find me a job."

"But you can do that anywhere, Edith."

"I ain't got no money."

"If you want I will lend you some."

She had me. I didn't want money from her! What had I come for? Why had I gotten on a train to wake up at her door? If I was splitting from Reverend Jenkins, why had I ended up in Peekskill?

123

"Mrs. Bates." I followed her back into the kitchen. "Did you know they found Bessie—dead?"

"Yes." She sure didn't waste pity. "Minnie told me. She took it very hard. I supposed you and Suzy did too."

"You saw Minnie?"

"Yes—shopping with Mrs. Cramer. Lovely girl, Minnie. Smart. Of your sisters she's the most like me."

True. That's what turned me off about Minnie. About Mrs. Bates. They both thought more about books than they thought about people. Minnie had cut out on Suzy without looking back. And as far as I was concerned, I didn't want to talk to her, didn't want to see her again. So what was I doing here? When I was away from her, I just never remembered how much Mrs. Bates bugged me.

"Thank God someone realized Minnie's potential and got her while she is still young," Mrs. Bates said.

"You don't think nothing of her going off to live with white folks?"

"We all have to give up something to get what we want, Edith. Remember that. Minnie might regret losing contact, her sense of blackness by not being around black folks. She might not. But whatever—she has to live with it. The important thing is that *she* made the choice. I happen to think it a wise choice."

Cold woman. Witch. Why had I asked her about Bessie? To get pity? I had been out of my mind. My eyes followed her as she walked out of the kitchen. Leaving me to what? My choice? "You outa it, lady," I mumbled as I went back into the room—my prison. "You really outa it. Since I seen you, I lost a home, a sister, I run back to you for some kinda feeling, and all you got is a story and some fucking books? Twenty damn dollars ain't give you that right."

I brushed the books off the desk. They landed on the floor with a loud plop that made me jump. Then I really got mad. I grabbed the pencils and broke them,

124

tore up the pads and scattered the paper over the floor. I pulled out drawers from the desk and banged them against the walls. Then I snatched my clothes, which she had hung in the closet, flung them in my suitcase, and stamped loudly through the kitchen, into the foyer. At the foot of the staircase I stopped, expecting to hear hurrying feet down the stairs, expecting to hear my name called, waiting for her to come down, try to stop me. Not one sound. Quiet had settled through the house. Hea—vy!

There was nothing to do but leave. I walked by the living room. Looked in. There she sat!

All that noise and she reading the newspapers! I stood staring at her. She turned a page. I breathed hard, moved my suitcase from one hand to the other. She knew I was standing looking at her! She turned another page. I fought against the devil not to rush her, tear the paper out of her hand, forcing her to look at me, say I didn't count. She turned another page.

I walked to the door. But someone rang the bell, banged at the door. "Open up. Open up. This is the law."

I stood there, waxed, my hand on the doorknob, refusing to turn it, refusing to fall off. "Open up in there, I say." My heart thudded against my chest, my mind kept saying, "Get away. Move. Hide." I stood, not moving.

"I know you in there," the man shouted. The banging kept on. Loud, louder. I held on to the doorknob to stop from falling.

Then Mrs. Bates was beside me. Silent. She held my arm, pulled me back through the foyer, back into the kitchen. She pushed me into my room, her face set, her eyes warning me to silence. She closed the door.

I stood at the door, my ear pressed against it, listening as she walked back through the kitchen, sounding her heels hard through the foyer. I heard the door open to the impatient caller. "Open up. Open up. Ain't I told you to open up this damn door and let the good law in?"

She laughed. Laughed! "My God," I heard her say. "Sometimes I do agree with Mr. Bates. James, you are a natural ass."

TWO

He walked through the house like a loud wind. "Damn, Aunt Martha, what took you so long? Never known you to be scared of no law. Whatcha putting down? Hell, if I'd stayed out there any longer I'd have turned into a statue outside that door. Now instead of a kiss you'd be having to chop me down."

Mrs. Bates kept laughing. "Can you believe it? James, I swear you have given me an education. I now know the exact location of my heart in my chest."

"Scared the hell outa ya, ain't I, old girl?"

"Didn't you?"

"Whatcha into? Come on, tell me. I want a piece of the action."

She knocked on my door, still laughing. "Come on out, Edith, and see what our good law looks like."

I slipped out of the room, shutting the door tight behind me so she didn't see the wreck I had made. I eased into the kitchen and away from the bedroom door, looking at him. God, he looked good. He wore a tan raincoat, brown sweater, and he was brown. Still Mr. Brown.

"No-o-o," he said. "That ain't what you been hiding. That ain't it at all. Hey there, pretty girl, you mean you been waiting for me all this time, sure 'nough? That's what I call fidelity. Come on, Dimples, give lover boy a kiss. Tell him how glad you is to see him."

I was. I burned all over with gladness. This time he had remembered me. Seemed so funny a guy—this good-looking guy—remembering me. Like I had remembered him. Thought about him. Things didn't happen like that twice for nothing. He knew I had come. Felt my presence. And so he had come. What other reason?

"Come on in the living room," Mrs. Bates said to him. "Tell me what you and my baby sister have been up to since I last saw you."

Back in my room I got busy stacking up the books, trying to piece back pencils, seeing which pages to keep from the torn pads. When I heard them go out of the house, I searched in the cellar, found a hammer, and went to work trying to fix the drawers I had broken. Then I looked into the books she had bought for me, wanting to see if it was possible to understand them.

I had to stay. To be near him, to be able to see him, I'd go along with any program she wanted.

I heard them come back. A little later Pops came. "Hey, Big Daddy." James greeted him. "Guess who's here?"

"I'll go back out, stay fifteen minutes, then maybe I won't have to."

"Ain't no way to talk, Marble Top. I'm here to spread out for a while. The only way you'll get rid of me is to start scraping at the corners."

"Will that do it? I guess I'd better start scraping right now," Pops said.

I hated for Pops to tease James like that. After all, James was an orphan. Mrs. Bates's older sister's child.

James had nobody but Mrs. Bates and the aunt he lived with in Harlem. Then I thought: the Bateses were the only folks I had, too. We were orphans together, James and me. That made me really settle down to the books.

At dinner Pops and James kept up their fooling. "What you want to bet," James said, "that this time around I'll stay two weeks?"

"Two weeks?" Pops almost shouted. "No, please. Spare me the pain."

"Horace, stop," Mrs. Bates said. "You know that this town is James's prison. After one turn around he'll be hotfooting it right back to Harlem."

"Is that a promise?" Pops asked with his lemon-twist smile.

"Of course. We have never been able to make him stay more than one day."

James winked at me, did a double-take at the look in my eyes. He reached under the table and rubbed my knees. A white-hot fire streaked through me. I looked at my plate. "Bet. Bet," he said. "Let your money support what your mouth is all about."

"A thousand dollars," she teased.

"Like you don't believe me, Aunt Martha. Don't you know the best things happen to me in the bosom of my family?" He kept running his hand on my leg.

"Anything that happens in your family," Pops said, "you'd know only by way of. If it's bad you'd never hear. If it's good—"

"Then I'll be there," James sang.

"You can say that again."

"Then I'll be there," he sang again.

They laughed, even Pops. Only they laughed at him, not hearing him. But his hand on my leg gave me the meaning behind his words. I didn't laugh. Only looked at my plate, breathing hard. Then he took his hand away and said, "You gonna be here, ain't you, baby?"

Hot and cold flushes confused my body. I didn't like

him bringing them in on our secret. Our feelings were sacred.

"Not your worry," Pops snapped.

Mrs. Bates laughed. "Edith hasn't really made up her mind if she's staying. She hasn't decided yet if the price I'm asking is too high."

She stood up. So did the others. They went on into the living room. I didn't. I sat, not moving. She had made things so hard.

She had let me know that she had heard me earlier. She knew I had been ready to leave. Knew why. She had not stopped me. Had had no intention of stopping me. She had made it clear: her way or no way.

I didn't want to go. I wanted to stay. But staying now meant begging. I didn't want to beg. In my room I took down the clothes I had just hung up, packed my suitcase again. But then I sat on the bed, James's touch still hot on my knees, my leg. Ashamed. I did not want to walk by the living room, suitcase in hand, letting him know that I was unwanted.

I heard their voices in the living room, talking, laughing, having a good time. I kept on sitting on the bed. Waiting. In a way I wanted Pops to come, or James—I wanted them to say to me, "Don't sit there all alone. Come where the action is. Come where we can see you—touch you." They kept talking. I kept sitting. After a while I got up and dressed for bed.

The next morning I dressed again, waited with the door closed for them to leave. They did. But I sat on the bed, not moving. Looking at my suitcase. I wanted to grab it, run, before anyone came back in. I kept looking at it. I didn't want to go. I lay back, staring at the ceiling until I fell asleep again.

Late that afternoon Mrs. Bates knocked at the door. "Edith, are you still busy?" I sat up. "I bought a

130

barbecued chicken for dinner," she said. "Come and give some suggestions on what we can have with it."

Nothing really to suggest. She had bought coleslaw, bread, and a green salad. I stood in the middle of the kitchen. Stupid. I wanted to help but didn't want her to stop me if I started.

"Why don't you set the table?" she suggested. I got busy with the plates.

"I didn't know if you'd still be here," she said, smiling. My mouth poked out. She laughed. "I'm glad you stayed. I do enjoy my nephew, but I like my girls better. Boys talk so much and say so little. Girls can say so much without opening their mouths."

That forced me to pull in my poked-out lips. She smiled. I grinned. She laughed. We laughed together. Yesterday fell to ashes. We had started over again.

THREE

From low I went to high. Laughing. Looking into
James's eyes and laughing. Feeling his leg reach for
mine under the table. Laughing. Seeing his eyes take
on two meanings—one for the Bateses and one for
me—and laughing. Seems I had won. Somewhere,
somehow, I had been playing a game I didn't know I
was playing and I had won. I had come here without
thinking. He had called me, and I had come. Here I
was in this house I loved, with the dude I dug the most
sitting next to me. Talk about telepathy? Wow. All I
had to do to keep things like this was a little reading,
a little studying. Hell, that was no sweat. And it
mightn't be for long. I sent questions deep into James's
eyes, and he nodded like he had read my mind and
agreed. I cracked up.

In the living room Pops and James got to drinking.
"Your old lady is really something," James said. "She
tried to get me back into the church today to hear the
choir practice."

132

"What did you do?" Pops asked.

"I let her dream. I found me a bar. Can you imagine listening to those hags singing and stomping on a Saturday night?"

"Lucky for the hags you found a bar," Pops cracked. I laughed.

"Horace." Mrs. Bates scolded. "James has outgrown those devilish ways."

"You mean rats stop eating cheese?"

"That's right, Big Daddy, don't you believe nothing good about me until you can prove it."

"You mean prove that a rat eats cheese?"

James winked at me. I cracked up.

I sat on the couch because I wanted to be near him. But he sat on the hassock near Pops's chair. I wanted to touch him, feel his hands on my knees, pretending it was accidental. It was impossible to go to him in the glare of that light. I went upstairs to the bathroom. Then I went into Debra's room and waited in the dark. Waited for him to come and touch me—just touch me.

He did come later. I heard him in the bathroom, and when he left, I slipped out of Debra's room and met him at the top of the stairs. "Hey there," he whispered. "Howya doing?"

I put my face up. He bent down and I grabbed the back of his head. Kissed him hard. "Well, now," he said, surprised. "Hold it now. Hold it for later."

Back down in the living room I kept laughing at Pops's and James's teasing, laughing at Mrs. Bates's smiling face, at her hands fingering her pearls. "It's one o'clock, Edith. Don't you think you and I should be going to bed?"

I floated to bed. I was higher than ever, happier than ever, listening to the clink of ice against glass as Pops and James kept on talking. Being happy was being where you wanted to be and knowing just what you wanted to do. Mrs. Bates sure was in for a surprise.

She had the smartest—but *the* smartest—pupil living in her house.

I heard him moving in the kitchen later—much later. But even sleeping I had been waiting. I saw the thin line of light under my door and kept looking at it even as I listened to the quiet of the house. Waited. My heart going wild against my chest. I saw the line widen. I looked up to see him framing the doorway, the light behind making a shadow of his face. Then my heart swoll, stopped me from breathing as he closed the door behind him.

He felt his way into the room, stumbling. His knees hit the bed, his hands felt along the bed for where I lay. Searched for my face. "Hey, there." he said. Heavy whiskey smell hit my face. "Come to say good night," he said.

I put on the bed lamp. "Hey, there you are." He stood wavering. Happy. "Ain't you glad I come to say good night?"

He leaned over. Kissed me. I put my arms around his neck, drew him down, kissing him back. "Hey, baby, you sure got some mighty fine lips there."

"Sh, they'll hear."

"Don't matter." But it did. It mattered to me. To him too. He whispered, "You sure kiss fine."

"We got to talk," I whispered back.

"Talk?" He sat on the edge of the bed. "What about, baby?"

"About us."

"What about us? Don't you dig me?"

"I love you."

"Well then." He pushed me back on the pillow. Kissed me. Kept kissing me. It got too serious.

"You better go now." I said.

"Go? Go where?"

"To bed."

"That's what I'm about, baby."

"What are you doing?" He had stood up and started unbuckling his pants.

"What it look like I'm doing?" He pulled off his pants. Sat back on the bed. "I want you, baby."

"I want you too. But not now. Not like this."

"How you sound?"

I wanted to tell him that I knew he needed me. That I needed him and that he didn't have to be just out there alone any more. Instead I said, "I ain't never done nothing like this before."

"Sure, sure. But it's got to be a first before there's another, right?"

"I don't want to."

"You don't what! What you think I hung around all day for? All that jive acting you been putting down? Hell, I'm splitting this scene. Ain't nothing I hate worse than a jive broad."

"I ain't jive," I said, hurt at his not understanding me.

"Can't prove it by me, baby."

"No. I swear. I ain't jive. Honest."

"Then take that thing off." He pulled down my nightgown straps .

"No."

"See what I mean? I don't know what you trying to pull, baby. But I ain't it." He pulled up his pants and went to the door.

"Don't go," I pleaded. We had so much to talk about. We were so much alike. If he left we might never talk about it again. "Please don't go."

He came back. "You gonna take that thing off?" I took off my nightgown. He pulled off his shoes, then slipped into bed next to me, under the covers. "I love you," I said.

"Yeah, and I'm crazy about you."

"Honest?"

"Sure. I'll prove it." He stripped off his clothes and

135

kicked them to the floor. Kissed my neck. I let him. He held me. The shock of his flesh against mine released me. I had never felt hot flesh against me. His arms were strong around me, and I knew this was the way folks were supposed to feel. Warm. Warm and together. Loving. Really, really loving. We orphans had sure found each other between earth and sky. Between earth and sky.

FOUR

For days. It was like losing sight of the world. I got to floating, flying, spaced out like the dudes on the moon. It was like losing sight on the world, me running and skipping, pulling down branches with reason to bloom come next spring. It was losing sight of the world when my mind got to churning, and I got to learning when learning or leaving was the stake. It sure was losing sight on the world when meaningful things got to losing their meaning.

"Edith, Suzy ran away from her foster home."

"Who said?"

"Minnie. She's been gone for days."

SuzyranawaySuzyranawaySuzyranawaySuzyranaway.

It was losing sight of the world being young. I'd never been young before. It was like losing sight of the world being happy. I had never been happy before. Losing sight of the world as my ears heard only words they wanted to hear.

"Got to git, baby. Go where the happenings is."

"But you promised to stay two weeks."

"Baby, we can't eat promises. Got to get the bread. Been here five days already. Got to hit the turf where the bread is in the works. Be back."

"When?"

"If I say when you'd be hot if I don't show. Be back, I say. Keep the faith. Ain't I got the sweetest thing going? The straightest aunt living. This is home, baby. You done made it home." It was losing sight of the world to believe and believe and believe when days became weeks and stretched into a month.

But then the world settles when waiting strains belief. And being young yesterday is being old today, and clouds harden into sidewalk under the feet. Then looking at the world is harder than coming down from the worst kind of high.

"Edith!"

"Ma'am?"

"Minnie wants to talk to you. Do you want to talk to her?"

"No, ma'am."

"It's only the two of you now . . ."

"Ma'am?"

"Suzy will show, of course. Somewhere. Sometime. But she's been missing for over a month now. Minnie really is worried."

"I can't talk to her."

James had been gone a month too. And nobody talked about him. Nobody wanted to talk about him.

"You can't keep holding her home against her. True, she's Minnie Cramer now. But she's still your sister."

But her cutting out on Suzy had made Suzy run away. I didn't answer. Mrs. Bates came to look over my shoulder. She saw the blank piece of paper I kept staring at. "You are under a terrible strain, Edith. You have done so well up to now. Maybe you need a rest." I still didn't answer.

She touched my hair. "Have you been giving any thought of where you go from here?"

To James, my mind said cold and clear. I had never been that clear about anything in my life. But why hadn't he come back? Why didn't he come?

When I still didn't answer, she picked up the book lying on the desk and flipped through it. "Are you having trouble with math?" I wanted her to leave, go away, let me think.

Pops came to the door. "What's happening?" he asked. "Conference? Need my help?"

"Edith is having trouble with math," Mrs. Bates answered. "You know that has always been my worst subject."

Pops came into the room, took the book from her, looked at it, looked into my face, then closed the book. "It's meanness beating a tired horse. Edith is tired, Mrs. Bates. What say we close up school until after Thanksgiving?"

Thanksgiving. My birthday. Eighteen years old and free. Only three more weeks. "Debra will be coming home," he said. "We won't have to worry about any books until December."

December? Another time started ticking inside of me.

Debra came home stuffed with college. "The work isn't really that hard. But the kids are the dumbest, brilliant kids I've ever seen. They know nothing—but so brilliantly."

The way she talked made me think of Minnie when we were living with Mrs. Peters and she first went to that mostly white school. Now I guess she talked that brilliant thing "brilliantly."

"There aren't many of *us* in that school," Debra said. "And those who are try so hard to be white they get self-conscious to be seen talking with other blacks.

139

There's one girl, though, a junior. I got to get to meet her. She's a real gone sister and together. Name's Daphne Duprey.''

Mrs. Bates kept smiling. Pops kept smiling. Letting her get her ''new thing'' off her shoulders. I kept waiting to get a burden off my mind. I didn't get her alone until after Thanksgiving.

''Debra, I think I'm gonna have a baby.''

''Baby?'' She laughed. ''Where in the world did you get the time with Mumsy on your back?'' When I didn't answer, she asked, ''Who's the boyfriend?''

''James.''

''James who?''

''James Edwards.''

''Where did— Who?''

''Your cousin.''

''You got to be kidding! When did all this happen?''

''He came in September.''

''Oh, then you got nothing but time. Did you tell Mumsy?''

''No! I don't want her to know.''

''For God's sake, why not? She ought to know.'' No, I didn't want Mrs. Bates ever to know the game I had been running on her. ''Mumsy's been on this fight to keep abortion legal for the longest.''

''Abortion! Debra, I don't want an abortion.''

It got to me. Her attitude. The most important thing in my life. It didn't matter to her.

''Don't tell me you want a baby?''

''Yes, I want my baby.''

''Edith, what for?'' She looked at me in disgust. ''Aren't you tired of taking care of babies?'' Then she never understood how much I loved babies. How much every one of them had meant to me. My sisters—the kids at The Institution. ''What about all this studying Mumsy said you were putting down? The plans for a diploma? A profession? You think all that will be easy with a baby?''

"Those ain't my plans. They your mother's."

"Ooooh?"

She looked and sounded like her mother then. Cold. Her look asked, "Then what are you doing here?" Aloud she said, "Mrs. Bates isn't really a mother. She's a force. She doesn't kiss and cuddle, and when she throws the truth at you it's a wallop. You either have it or you don't." Then she gave a quick hitch to her shoulders. "I think it's wild. But it's your baby. Go on and have it."

Funny how I thought we had been together against her mother. She sure had told her things I had wanted to. But looking now into her wide, honest eyes glancing around her room, loving things, I saw that her thinking had changed in just those few months at college.

"Look, I didn't lie to your mother." I defended. "I—she just threw it up to me. I had to go along." Because of James. I had to get to know him. Had to be near him. Aloud I said, "But you don't have to worry. I'm leaving your house."

"For God's sake, Edith. What's that all about? Where will you go?"

"To the city. To James—"

"What! What good will that do?"

"We—we sorta like one another. We—I guess we'll get married."

"Who? James?" She stared at me. "You out of your mind, Edith? Marry? Throw that thought out of your head. James isn't going to marry you. He's not going to marry anybody."

She sat on the edge of the bed and looked at me as though trying to think of how best to get through to me.

"You don't really know James," I said. "You don't understand him."

Her eyes probed mine, tried to look into me. I didn't let her. "James is my cousin," she said. "I was born knowing him. And he being the way he is has nothing

141

to do with my feelings for him. James has been out there. He's had his kicks and bruises. That does funny things to some men.

"Look, tell Mumsy. She mightn't like it, but she'll deal with it. Kids in my school go down to New York every weekend for abortions. They come back and keep right on with their studies. Men might knock us up but they no longer knock us out, Edith. This is not the Middle Ages."

She left the room and ran down the stairs, long, lean, full of life and her new thinking. Like her mother she had given me her advice. And just like that my feeling for her had changed.

FIVE

I got off the train in Harlem, walked up 125th Street, and walked back into yesterday. The crowds of folks on the streets were thick and busy because of the start of the Christmas shopping season. And even in the cold, groups stood around on corners stomping heat into their blood, smoke blowing out of their noses, laughing loud and making like it was already Christmas. I walked slow to remember. I passed the movie houses I used to sneak into, the Chock Full o'Nuts. They had boss cream pies. The Woolworth, where I used to do my sleight-of-hand to make objects disappear and where Phyllisia and I had got caught in a riot, had already put up its Christmas wreath. On the other side of the street, the agency with its sign: DAYS WORK, MAIDS, CHAUFFEURS, HANDYMEN. I had sat for hours there after my old man blew, waiting for the day's work jobs.

Home again? I sure knew the place. I had passed even the house where I was headed dozens of times when I was growing up around Harlem. James might have been living there then—with his Aunt Mary, Mrs. Bates's baby sister. His mother might have died in one of these houses just like Phyllisia's mother had—like my mother had.

I had walked past Lenox Avenue. Now I walked back and turned down the avenue, heading downtown. Still walking slow. Looking around the streets for him now. Wanting to see him. Praying to see him. It seemed right that he bring me home to meet Aunt Mary. I walked slow, reached his block. No sign of him. Not too many people out in the wind, away from the shopping center. Still hoping, I came to his house.

My suitcase got heavy as I pulled it up the stoop. I put it down and waited. Listened to the sounds of the house: dogs barking, stereos playing, babies crying, and naturally loud-talking folks. I pushed the frame of the glassless door, climbed the one flight of stairs to the apartment with the outline of a missing five. This was the address I had found in Mrs. Bates's address book.

I rang the bell. No sound. Knocked. Listened. Knocked harder. A shuffling of feet. Soft. I knocked harder. The shuffling became footsteps. Slid to the door. "Who is it?"

"It's me."

"Me? Who?"

"Edith."

"Edith who?"

"Edith Jackson."

"Who Edith Jackson?"

"Miss Mary, I—I just come down from Peekskill."

"Peekskill?" The door opened. A suspicious, large red-veined eye looked through a crack.

"Whatcha want?"

"Edith Jackson?" I looked for interest. None. "I—I live with Mrs. Bates."

"Oh, why ain't you said so? Come on in." Tall woman and almost as broad around. She heaved to one side to let me in. Her fat shook. "Ain't heard a no gal living up there

144

with Martha. But them folks don't never tell me nothing. They don't call. . . ."

My gaze fumbled away from her face, past her hanging other chin. I looked at her big belly and on down to her heavy legs, thick ankles, and wide feet stuck into the broken-down backs of a pair of men's shoes, the heels dragging on the floor behind. I turned to look over the kitchen I had walked into. But the sink piled with dishes, the table with crumbs reminded me of another time—of my home in Harlem—so I looked back at her face where kindness creased the soft rolls of fat.

"Never come. Only time I hears is when James goes up there. Know James?" I nodded. I know James. But *you* don't know Edith? Edith Jackson? Ain't he never called that name?

"I—I come to see James."

Hot blood rushed up at the quick business her eyes gave me—my suitcase. "All the way down here to see James? Martha send him word—or something?"

"No—no. I—I just got to see him."

The fat held still. Eyes jumped wise—street-wise. Something inside them backed away. Cloudy eyes got shifty. "We—el, guess he be in directly." Then she made a don't-care with her shoulders. "Nigger stays out in the streets." Her eyes turned to a clock ticking loud on the kitchen shelf. "Lord, four o'clock already. Done slept my figger."

Dragging heavy legs, she moved toward the door leading to the rest of the apartment. "Just drop that bag of yourn—anywhere. Ain't no sense in just standing there hanging on to it. He'll be in directly." Another drag toward the door, she stopped. "You sure Martha ain't sent word to me?" Shook my head. She wiggled her shoulders again, heaved over the doorsill. "Set down. He'll be back. In and out. Out and in. That's him. Don't know nobody what loves the streets like that boy." The dark of the inner house reached out and closed her in.

I sat holding my hands, not wanting to disturb the roaches greasing on the crumbs and dried egg yolk on the table. Sat there until the darkness pushed her back out. This time she wore a coat she tried hard to make meet over her belly.

"Got to run out," she said. "But make yourself to home. Be right back." Her fat heels still wiped up the floor. "If's something you want, look around. James'll be in. In and out. Out and in, that's him." A sigh helped her out the door.

I sat staring at the door, not believing. Not knowing what I didn't believe. I tried not to think. Stop up my mind. But some black eyes kept poking at me. I said aloud, "Y'all sure's some tall folks." In my ears I heard, "Oooooh?"

Four-thirty. A loud-ticking clock. Kept thinking. In and out. Out and in. Didn't like the sound of her words. Most people didn't dig James. Like Debra, Pops—even his aunt? Orphans sure had a lone road to go.

The clock ticked. Hot. Took off my coat. Held it in my lap. Five o'clock. Waiting. Like I spent my life waiting. That simple old clock—God, sure was loud.

On the streets—these streets—things happened. Folks got hit by cars; folks got shot—killed; folks got stabbed—died. Anything might happen to him out there. Dead out there in the cold, cold streets. Naw. I wanted that simple clock to stop. I looked at it. Kept looking. Five-thirty. Five-thirty-one. Five-thirty-two. Five-thirty-three. . . .

Someone fumbled at the door. My eyes shifted. A key. Looked at the lock. Quiet. I held my breath. Then the door shot open, shut with a slam. Then—there he walked, through the kitchen, fast. Walked right past me into the other room. Quiet. Loud kinda quiet. Liked to crack my eardrums. Then he backed out. Backed out until he had gone back past the table. Open-mouthed. He stared.

SIX

"Hey. Hey, whatcha know? Ann? Judy?" He snapped his fingers, hit his leg. "Hey, naw—Peekskill, ain't it? Aunt Martha . . ."

Always joking. Looking for a laugh. But folks didn't joke that way. Hurting jokes. "Long way for a kid to be traveling, huh? Alone?"

I nodded. What kid did he mean? This eighteen-year-old? Mother-to-be-of-his-baby? His girl. A kid?

"I—I had to see you."

"Me? What about?" His eyes shifted to the suitcase.

"I— I— It's important."

Shifty eyes. I hadn't remembered them shifty. "Sure, sure, look. I ain't got the time right now, see? Where you staying? I'll be around, you dig? We'll talk awhile, you dig?

"I—I—Please. It's important."

He moved back to the front door. I jumped up. "No!" In and out. Out and in. Hours to wait. "No— look. Don't you *want* to see me?"

147

"Sure, sure, baby. But you know how it is. I got this dude to meet. . . ."

I hadn't come to beg. I swallowed at the thickness starting in my throat. Swallowed hard. Then, quick, to keep him from leaving: "I—I'm gonna have a baby."

"Mine!" Quick snap of his fingers. "That's right. You was a virgin. I remember. I sure do. Came right home and wrote it down in Aunt Mary's Bible. First virgin I ever had. That means I got to marry you—right?"

My knees gave way from relief. He wanted to marry me. What did Debra know? Not a thing. I wanted to smile. Make dimples. My face just trembled. "Aunt Martha know?" he asked. I shook my head. "And you ain't said nothing to Aunt Mary, is you?" I shook my head again. "Well, ain't no sense telling till we do it. That old lady talks like a parrot. Where you staying?" I shook my head; I had nowhere to go. "Well, first thing we finds you a place, right?"

I wanted to say no. I wanted to stay here with Aunt Mary—a line to Mrs. Bates, Pops. But James had grabbed my suitcase, took hold of my arm. "Let's get the hell outa here."

I trotted to keep step with him. He raced. I kept trotting, keeping faith. Praying. Why pray? Everything settled. Happy ever after. And praying? Trotting to get a promise kept. A promise? "Where we going?"

"To find us a place, baby." Why had I asked? He had told me already. And his feet raced toward well-known places. The corners they turned were not strange to him. His racing head, straining, like a horse to the finish line. I had never known that look about him. And because I had never seen him like that, a worm of fear tickled my back. I tried to disown it. But this place where I had spent all my life, the place I had grown up in, fought in, gone to school in, looked strange.

Dark, cavelike places took shape in my mind, growing as he kept moving. Giant shadows, spread eagle-like against buildings. Loud laughter, loud curses hit against the stone walls, bounced against my ears. I trotted on. Kept trotting, keeping up.

Finally we turned into an alley. Went down a flight of steps into a court made by the windowless side walls of two buildings and the back of a third. We went through the court, and James tapped out a code on the door of the third building. The door opened and a big black man stood in the doorway, the light from behind him outlining a headful of braids.

"Hey, Stu." James laughed that old loud laugh. "I brung us some company. Figgered we might use a li'l cheering up 'round here. This here is Edith. Just blew into town—right, Edith? Thought you might have a li'l space we can crawl into and spread out. Know what I mean?"

"Sure thing." The man called Stu stepped aside. We went into this low-ceilinged basement. "Always got a place for my ole buddy." Stu smiled, exposing broken, tobacco-stained teeth. "But she mighty young, ain't she?"

"When they young, you don't go wrong," James sang. They cracked up. "Where we parking, Stu?"

"Right on in the back, Jimmy boy."

We walked past three bedrooms and a kitchen before getting to the back room—a messed-up room with a dresser, a bed with lumps like hills, a table with a setup of whiskey glasses on a tray.

"Don't worry 'bout a thing, baby. My man Stu will look out for you, dig? He the janitor here. He don't never mind doing me favors, you know?"

I kept staring at him, trying to see the James I knew in Peekskill. He didn't even resemble that man, Mr. Brown. His face didn't belong in clean places—sure not the same house with Mrs. Bates, Debra, Pops. It belonged in that apartment with Aunt Mary or here, in this shadowy house with its damp air, its dirty bed.

"James." I called his name to hear his voice. See if he answered. He did.

"Yeah, baby, everything's cool. Everything's under control, right?" I wanted to run. Kept remembering I had come down to *marry him*.

He set my suitcase down and right away got to undressing.

"What are you doing?" I whispered.

"What's it look like I'm doing, baby?"

"Ain't we gonna talk?"

"Talk? About what, baby?"

"About us. About what we gonna do."

"What's more to talk about? You say you pregnant. I say we get married. What more?"

He came to me. Kissed me. I strained inside to feel the same as in Peekskill. Got scared instead. Pulled away.

"What's happening, baby?"

"I don't want to. Not till we get married."

"What?" He looked me up and down. "Oh, till we get married? Okay." He pulled on his shirt. Slipped into his coat and moved to the door.

"Where you going?"

"Out. You got to be hungry. Gonna get us some grits, okay?" He walked out.

I kept staring at the closed door. Tried it. Found it opened. He had gone for food. I looked out the window. Bars separated it from the court. I sat on the bed. Dim lights made bad shadows. Better to be in darkness. I sat. Time passed. I waited, ticking off time to the beat of the clock in Aunt Mary's kitchen. Waited.

The door opened and Stu walked in. Cramped up the small room. Standing over me, he sucked me into his shadow. "Whatcha want?" I whispered.

"Whatcha mean what I want? Get on in bed. A deal's a deal." He reached for me. I scrambled to the other side of the bed. He grinned, showing off his brown teeth. He ran around the bed, pulling at his shirt. He threw me across the bed, started unbuckling his belt. I screamed. Screamed. He put his hand over my mouth.

"Hey, what you want to go and do that for? I ain't hurt yer. I ain't about to hurt yer."

He took his hand away. I kept screaming. He put it back. "For God's sake, quit that. Folks'll think I'm killin' yer. If you don't want to—just say so. I ain't gonna force yer. I ain't never forced a broad in my life."

I looked into his big, anxious face. Looked down at his rough, scratchy hands. Looked up at his braided hair. And I choked back the screams. "What you come here for, anyway?" he asked.

"I'm gonna have a baby. Am gonna have a baby am gonna have a baby." The words kept repeating themselves. "Am gonna have a baby."

"Hey, come down. Come down. Easy now. Easy." His big rough hands shook my shoulders, kept shaking. "Calm down, li'l girl. "

"But I'm gonna have a ba—by." The puzzle in his strange-looking face made me swallow, only this time the lump burst. Crazy choking sounds came tearing out with this flood of water. I gritted my teeth to keep holding them, but they spurted out—ugly, funny sounds—and all this water, spilling out, drowning my face, falling down over his hands. I kept looking into his face, blurring through the flood, changing like a face in a funny mirror. Let it out. I hadn't cried for the old man. I hadn't cried for Bessie. I hadn't cried for Suzy. I cried now. I wanted to and so I let it come.

And he let me. This man Stu. He let me, like he knew I had to. Had to grieve. For all my hurt. My pain. For all the things past. Clearing myself for the future.

"Am gonna have a baby. *Hmmm.*" Moaning, rocking, suffering. *"Hmmm. A baby. A baby."*

"For Jimmy boy? Jesus Christ, for Jimmy boy?

Lord, no, not for him," he kept saying to keep time with my moaning. Like his words went with my moaning. "Hell, what you want to do a fool thing like that for? Not for Jimmy boy. Jesus Christ, not for him." He put his arm around my shoulders. Big arm. Big awkward arm. "That weren't smart. Sure not. He ain't nice. Not to me neither. Paid him. Yes, suh. Paid him good money. Sure weren't a nice thing he done—you with a baby and all. God be damn."

Later, in his old kitchen, we sat together, sipping tea. He said, "Go on back home, li'l girl. Go tell your folks. Hell, you ain't the first somebody been knocked up by a no-good man. It been happening since 'fore the Virgin Mary. It'll sure be happening long till Kingdom time comes. The wors' part's in the tellin'. But by the time the li'l one comes, lovin' it's gonna make that part long forgot. Go on back home, gal. New York ain't no place for a sweet gal like you."

But I had been born here. Come up here. My sisters and me. I didn't belong in Peekskill. Nor to the Bateses. James belonged to them. They knew him. Had known him. Had forgiven him for being Jimmy boy long before I had known him—known them.

I got up to leave. Stu fumbled in his pocket and brought out a handful of money. Counted ten dollars— all of it. "Ain't tell you what to do. But take this and go on home, gal. Go on home."

SEVEN

"Okay, step up. Step up. You there, don't hold up the line"

"He talking to you." Someone touched my back, and I inched up in the line. "Coffee and doughnut, please."

Four in the morning and folks, folks, in that all-night cafeteria. Partying folks on their way home or out to party some more. I took the coffee and doughnut and went to my corner table. I sat, waiting for dawn.

Still cold from my night walk through the streets, I sipped coffee, looking around the cafeteria to see a face I knew. Not one. Not one somebody, in this place I belonged, to say "Hiya" or "Welcome back" or "How long since you been gone?" This had been my home, hadn't it?

A man shouted in the telephone booth near my table, "Hey, baby, I'm on my way over. You needing me?. . . What?. . . What time is it? Baby, no such

153

thing as time. Just events and circumstances. Be right there."

Thought of Mrs. Bates. Of calling her and saying, "Four o'clock. Ain't no such thing as time. Just events and circumstances." Event: out in the street. Circumstance: having a baby. I giggled. Looked up into the face of a woman who thought I was smiling with her. She smiled back. We kept looking at each other.

She was flashy looking. Pretty under that flash. All her make-up didn't hide that she had smooth black skin, and the heavy mascara pointed up the sexy droop of her lashes over her frog eyes. We kept looking at each other, and she got up and came toward me. Plump, with a fur coat—fox, I guess—and high-heeled shoes, with cobwebby stockings.

"I know you," she said.

"Me?

"Yeah, you Edith, ain't you?"

Just like that I remembered her. "Beulah?"

"Yeah." She sure looked good. In school we had called her Big-Tits. But she had grown to it—plump all around and pretty. She had a long wig that made her look different from the tough chick I used to warn off my friend Phyllisia.

"I thought you lived in the sticks," she said. "Saw your friend. She told me."

"Yeah, Phyllisia told me she saw you. Sure was glad to see you."

"Me too. She sure growed pretty. You, you look the same."

Seeing that I had the same clothes as when I left Mother Peters' in Peekskill and that my eyes must look a mess from crying, I didn't know if she meant that as a compliment. "You don't," I said. "You sure have changed. Looking sharp."

"Whatcha doing here?"

"Keeping warm."

"In here? This ain't no time for squares to be warming in this joint."

"Waiting for light to get to Phyllisia's."

"Why you gotta wait for light?"

"Her old man, you know. He ain't gonna dig nobody ringing his bell so early."

"Her old man? Shee—it. Look, don't you be staying out here in the streets. I got a pad. My friend over there and me, we share it. Give us a buzz. Stay as long as you like." She took a pencil from her bag and wrote on a napkin. "My address. Give us some time to get rid of them squares and come on." I glanced at her address. She lived on the same avenue—Eighth Avenue—as my old neighborhood, except farther downtown, nearer Central Park.

She closed her bag, dipped into her brassiere, pulled out a roll of bills, peeled off ten dollars and threw it on the table. "Buy yourself another cup of coffee while you waiting." She went back to her flashy friend, and right away they got to loud talking and laughing.

I slipped her address in my coat pocket, feeling better. Seeing her, remembering her, how she beat up my friend, Phyllisia, how I had taken her on—even though she had always been bigger than me—gave me a link to old times, made me feel at home. I sat there thinking and smiling, smiling. . . .

"Hey, how about some grits, my man?"

Shouts woke me. Big men were lining up at the steam tables: truck drivers, policemen, bus drivers, men with big appetites—the hard workers. "Bacon and eggs, looking at yer," the counterman yelled. I ordered another cup of coffee. The night crowd—including Beulah and her friends—had disappeared.

Seven o'clock. I left the cafeteria, took a bus to Phyllisia's street, walked the three blocks to the tree-lined street where Phyl lived. The brownstones across from her building still had that special, cared-for look. Even the dead gardens fronting them had been raked, and some had artificial green imitating until next spring. The apartment-house side of the street showed the start of a struggle. The doors were standing open, and graffiti were scrawled over the outside of the buildings.

I stood for a long time looking into the lobby of Phyllisia's apartment house, remembering her father. I didn't see his face, only his bigness and the big shadow he cast when he entered a room. I didn't know him except for his meanness. The sound of his loud voice kept filling my head, stopping up my ears. Why had I come? To his house?

Phyl had said he had changed. But I hadn't heard from her in so long—over a year. How did a man like Calvin change? But then he might not remember me. It had been a long time ago. And now my coat was no longer ragged, my stockings had no holes, my shoes were not turned over at the heels. I might not be Miss Park Avenue, but I'm no ragamuffin. Not any more. No ragamuffin.

I pushed open the door, walked up the three flights of stairs, and stood listening at their door. What code might bring her to the door? Her or her sister, Ruby?

I stood there listening, listening. I turned away. Started down the stairs. A baby cried. I came back. Rang the bell. A baby? In Phyllisia's house?

Footsteps sounded up the long hall on the other side of the door. The baby yelled. "Who's there?" a woman asked.

"Me."

"Me who?"

"Edith."

"Who?"

"Edith Jackson."

"Whatcha want?"

"Phyllisia. I come to see Phyllisia."

"Ain't no Phyllisia here." The baby screamed. The

footsteps ran back down the hall inside. Harlem folks sure were a scared bunch when it came to opening doors.

Looked at the door. I had only been there once. Maybe the wrong apartment. I went downstairs. A man was about to leave, locking his door. "Mister, do you know Phyllisia Cathy?"

"Nope. Don't know that name."

"Or Ruby—two real pretty girls. Father owns a restaurant on—"

"Oh, them. Big guy used to live over me. Had him a restaurant on Seventh Avenue."

"Yes, that's them."

"Yeah, had some girls—thought they could fly."

"Suh?"

"Yeah, something wrong with them girls. One come out the back window, try to come in my window."

"Flying?"

"She had taken off to fly. But she was just hanging there by a sheet. Took her in, and she wants to give me a hard time."

"What happened to them? They moved?"

"Yeah. Hear he give up his restaurant too. Don't never see him. Don't know why he closed." Then he shook his head again. "Them girls was somethin'." He kept shaking his head, like that was the strangest thing ever to happen.

Back down on the stoop, I sat, disappointed, not surprised. I guess I'd have been surprised to find them. Disappointment was my life. I sat looking at folks coming in and leaving that building, the houses up and down the streets, seeing the cars pulling out. Then after a time the streets got empty. It was still cold, but the wind had died down, so I sat, planning.

I'd go around my old block, leave my suitcase with my old grocer, then look around. For what? Work? Better go to Welfare. I had no place to live. Pregnant, and twenty dollars in my pocket. Somebody had to do something until I found work. I walked up to Eighth Avenue.

At the sight of my old block my bladder got right weak and my bowels got shaky: Fire, like one of them monsters restored from the past, had raged through the buildings on either side of my old building, right down to the grocer's store. And it was the same all around. Like a great blight, the monster, fire, had struck, leaving buildings standing untouched only here and there.

But the winos still crunched together at the corners, counting change for their first half-pint. And the junkies, spaced out, still nodded all along the sidewalks. But now alley cats marched in and out of the gutted buildings, like, serving notice, they were taking over.

Spaced out, too, by the sight, I stood across the street, staring up at the top floor of the building where I had lived with my family. The bricks of that building were blackened with smoke. But people still lived there. I saw faces pressed against the window, looking out into the street.

And as I looked, the window grew larger, came closer to the street so that I found myself staring into the weak eyes of an old man. Papa! And behind him, Randy stood grinning, just grinning. Then screams, loud screams came from somewhere. Baby Ellen's! I put up my hands to stop up my ears. Then I saw Bessie, staring at me, her big eyes growing bigger, spreading out like sunflowers, spinning and spinning, leaving the window, heading straight for me.

I split the scene. Moving like the wind, my suitcase hitting against my legs, trying to trip me. I kept putting distance between them and me, and when I saw a bus keeping time with me, I jumped on and made it down the avenue to Beulah's part.

But the blight that had hit uptown Harlem was nothing compared to what had happened to this part of the avenue. These old buildings had caved in on themselves, crushed by some giant forces. Wiring hung loose in the bombed-out insides of buildings. Plaster, wood, cement, dust dripped like slow-falling rain. Where once there had been stores or ground-floor apartments, slabs of concrete lay, every which way. And on those slabs of concrete, addicts rode, diving from the crumbling top floors, down into cellar caves, on the hanging wires and cables, then up again. Spook tunnels. Kids slid down wire ropes, from the shaking walls of upper floors down into the street; others ran in and out of the cluttered ruins, playing, dodging the rain of plaster and dust. Still others rolled down the mountains of garbage, piled two stories high, rotting— garbage where rats pushed out heads as big as cats' and fought with dogs for their meals.

Beulah's building stood solid, though, in the middle of the block. Folks kept coming in and going out. Dark-brown-skinned gays with dyed blond hair and blue eyes spread out their capes—Superman fashion—and flew to the upper floors into the waiting arms of jazzy chicks, dressed in furs, with big, broad laughing painted faces.

Then out of a garbage heap one rat ran toward me, skinning its teeth. Bessie's eyes stared out of its head. I saw Ellen this time, riding a concrete block, grinning. Trying to get that one together, I noticed this gang of boys walking toward me. And there in the center, their leader, Randy again! The ground held my feet as they walked up. But when Randy reached out for me, to pull me to him, I tore my feet up. Flew. Kept flying. Getting away.

Out of breath, I looked around. Old familiar Central Park. Beautiful park. Unsafe park. The park where Phyllisia and I had come to talk when we were young. I pulled my suitcase behind me, searching for the spot which we had called *our* spot.

We had talked about things here. Talked about telepathy. And it seemed right that I had come, chased by ghosts.

I put my suitcase under a tree, closed my eyes, and concentrated. "Phyllisia, Phyllisia, come. I need you. I need you. . . ." I waited for answering vibes. None. "Phyllisia, Phyllisia, come. Come. I need you. I need you. . . ."

Boys running across the open field broke the spell. The smell of hot dogs and sauerkraut hit my nostrils. I jumped up, ran after the boys to a pushcart standing in the lane above.

I ordered two. "Put everything on it," I told the old, wrinkled man with kind eyes.

"You looka hongry," he said.

"Sure am." I grinned. "Ain't eaten for days."

"Whata matta? You no gotta money. . . ." Suspicion took over his smile.

"Sure, got lots a money." I showed him the ten.

"Whata you do? Run away?" He pointed to my suitcase, looking lonely under the tree.

"Who me? I'm eighteen."

"No, you no gotta eighteen." He shook his head. "Fourteen, en maybe. No gotta eighteen. I bet is a boy. You can tella me. You fall inna love. I know."

"Another hot dog. More sauerkraut."

A boy? A man? I tried to think of James's face. Funny. I had never ever been able to see his face unless he was right there on the scene. Always remembered the brown jacket, the brown skin, the tan shirt. His face? Never.

Eating the hot dog, I tried to take the face apart. The eyes: no expression. The nose? He had one. Not flat, not high. Not easy to remember. His mouth? Teeth? He did so much laughing, and I didn't remember the teeth. I remembered the head, pushing like a horse trying to get somewhere.

The old man kept looking at me. I shook my head. "I come to meet a friend. A girl."

"And she notta come? Why? You run away?" He kept pointing to the suitcase.

"She don't know I'm here. You see, I'm trying to reach her through mental telepathy. You know mental telepathy?"

"No. What this menta'?"

"You see, we used to play here when we was kids. Me and this friend. So I concentrate real hard—like this."

I shut my eyes and mumbled, "Phyllisia, Phyllisia, I need you."

I opened them. "You see? She's supposed to hear and come."

"Why you notta go to her house?"

"I did. But she moved. You see, I live out of town—"

"You notta bringa this rabbit foot?"

"A what!"

"Thisa rabbit foot you colored believe, no? Is a rabbit foot. That bringa more quick."

That got me hot. "Look, you can keep your hot dogs. Gimme my change."

I walked away without looking back.

"Hey," he called. "And thisa friend—she not gotta telephone? Name in book? Thatta better than a rabbita—no?"

I stared at him pushing his pushcart. "Smartass," I called. But by that time he had gone too far to hear.

EIGHT

They called it a high rise, the building where Phyllisia
lived, looking down on Harlem.

"Whatcha want here?" The doorman barred my way
in the lobby.

"I come to see my friend."

"What friend?" He was eyeing me, suspicious.

"Phyllisia Cathy."

"You wait here. What's your name?"

"Edith. Edith Jackson."

Uncomfortable. I stood still. Didn't want to brush
against the marble tile or the mirrors or large plants
decorating the lobby. Busy lobby. Men and women
coming and going. Elderly women with smart haircuts,
taking out their fancy dogs. Younger women and men,
sharp, with their Listerine smiles, their fashion-book
clothes.

I kept looking at them, wanting to nod, smile. But
they walked by like they walked through me, not seeing
me. That got to me. I should have telephoned instead

of trying to surprise her. Surprised myself. My neat clothes felt like rags, compared to the clothes on these folks.

If Calvin Cathy walked in the lobby, he might not know me. But if he opened the door upstairs? Ragamuffin.

"Hey, you." I jumped. "Go on up, Sixteen C."

The elevator shot upward too fast to think. When the brain got to working, I thought of another elevator down. But when I got off, Phyllisia stood there waiting for me.

"Edith! What are you doing in New York?" She hugged and kissed me. Looked at my suitcase. "Oh, you came to spend some time."

Her happy-to-see-me face made me feel real again. Like people again. But when she pulled me into the apartment and I looked around at the grand living room with the browns and greens splashed with orange, the paintings on the walls, the live plants, the shadow of her father took over, and I stood waiting to see him come out, to hear his loud voice.

"It's so weird, your coming today," Phyllisia said. "I swear I got up this morning thinking of you. I kept wanting to go out and walk around, thinking I might bump into you or something."

"You did!" It worked, old man. It worked. "I tried to reach you through telepathy. You know, like we used to talk about? I went by your old place and this man said you had moved. I didn't know what else to do. I went to the park."

"The park? For all I know I might have found myself there if Ruby hadn't locked me in today, pretending she's sick."

"Ruby?" I had thought Ruby dead. Why? "Ruby's all right?"

Phyllisia waved her hands. Impatient. "Sure, she's all right, but she's acting sick. You know how she is?"

I smiled. Phyllisia sure didn't change. Not her ways.

163

Not her looks too much. She still had a little-girl face. She had let her Afro haircut of two years before grow out, and she had it twisted in some way on top. But in her jeans and T-shirt, she did have the figure of a young lady. And that made things strange.

I looked out the window to a playground across the street and saw children playing, like bugs, cars flying up and down the broad avenue without one sound. Unreal. All that noise out there, and in here as much noise as flies pissing on bread.

"Why did I think Ruby was dead, Phyl?"

"What? Sh, don't let her hear that. It will give her ideas. You must be talking about the letter I wrote about her *trying* to kill herself. Over some simple thing. She never made it clear. But that's long ago. I wrote to you since. You never answered. Why?"

"I haven't gotten any letters since that one. I—I—I'm not with Mrs. Peters."

"No? Who are all you with?" Still her West Indian talk. "Where are the children?"

"Bessie is—Minnie is—" Too much to tell. "So Ruby is still—But you must have a lot to tell me. Why didn't you tell me you were moving?"

"I wrote. I kept writing. Daddy sprang that on us right after that Ruby thing. He just packed us up and—"

"The man downstairs, in your old house, said you all left a long time ago. That your old man closed down his place—"

"Yeah. Just before he died—"

"Died? Your old man's dead!"

A wild wind rushing through darkened the room, bringing all my fears together in my chest like a fist. I pulled myself in on the couch, hardly breathing. When I opened my eyes, I looked straight into Phyllisia's secret smile. "See, Edith? I'm an orphan too. Now I'm an orphan just like you."

Like that was meant to bind us. Tie us together for

164

life. But the apartment, all its rich stuff, laughed at her exaggeration. She might be an orphan but sure not like me.

"Edy, can you imagine anybody so mean and evil actually dying?"

"He left y'all pretty straight. What happened to him?"

She shifted her eyes, hitched her shoulders. "This apartment is not ours. This belongs to Cora—"

"Cora—"

"Phyllisia, who's in there with you?"

"That Ruby, she's so nosy. She feel she must know everything."

That secret-best-friends-together way made her Phyllisia. Made me at home. But I wanted to see Ruby. "Why don't we just see how she is and get it over with?" I said.

Propped up in bed, wearing yellow, Ruby was prettier than I had remembered. Her skin a velvet brown, her eyes still see-through brown. "Do I know you?" she asked.

"Edy," Phyllisia snapped.

"Edith, God, you did grow. The last time I saw you, you were little."

"I'm eighteen."

"True. True. Phyllisia will be eighteen in a few months. You kids don't remain kids long."

"You must be twenty," I reminded her.

"Yes."

We were all grown—of age. Strange. I kept thinking of us sitting around her dying mother. At that time I had seemed the oldest.

"What about your sisters?"

What about them? "Minnie's—she's the bright one—she's way ahead in school."

Why hadn't I told them about Bessie? Suzy? Why hadn't talkative Phyllisia told me about what Calvin had died from? Everything had to wait its time.

"How long are you staying?" Ruby asked.

"A long time," Phyllisia answered.

"How long?"

"How long are you staying, Edith?"

"I—I don't know."

"At least a week," Ruby insisted. "Mother won't be back for another week."

"Mother?" I looked at Phyllisia.

"She's talking about Cora, my father's wife. I wrote you about Cora. He willed her to us."

"Phyllisia." Ruby's eyes flashed angrily.

"Well, didn't he? You act like I'm lying."

"If he hadn't, where do you think you'd be now? Out in the streets."

I looked from Ruby, pretty in her yellow, to Phyllisia, with her long legs and strange ways, her singsong West Indian accent. Shook my head. Not true. Not in the streets, these two. Life may be hard for them but never like for me.

Somehow, somewhere, at some time, someone had decided—before we were even born—that some orphans lived in places like this, while others lived in The Institution.

Phyllisia kept making head signs: let's go. I pretended not to see. I wanted to be with Ruby. Her feeling-sorry eyes warmed me. I had to talk to somebody, and I wanted it to be her. But Phyllisia walked to the door and stood waiting. Jealous. She *was* my best friend. I had to go.

"Ruby is simple," she burst out the second we were out of the room. "Always grateful. Always loving. I'm not. Calvin married Cora just so he could have someone to look after her. She pretending she's killing herself. I tell you they drive me mad! I'm running away."

"Running away?"

"Yeah. That Cora is worse than my father. I hate her."

Phyllisia always had to hate somebody and love

166

somebody. She didn't have her father. Now she hated her stepmother. She still loved me, and so I didn't tell her that at eighteen she didn't have to run away. All she had to do was move.

"Why do you hate her?"

"She's always telling us what to do and what not to do. Ruby doesn't mind. I do. I don't need anybody telling me what to do." Then her face lit up. Excited. "Edy, I'm so glad you came. You can run away with me. We—some kids from the university and—"

"What university?"

"NYU—and me—we're going to hitch rides out to California. You know this Route Sixty-six? Well it runs from New York straight to California. We can have a ball."

I sidestepped that dream. "What's with Ruby?" I asked. "She been sick long?"

"Ruby? No. Nothing's the matter with her. She only had an abortion."

NINE

I had never been able to keep up with Phyllisia talking.
I never tried. I didn't try now. I lay in bed and listened.
Or pretended to as she kept it up across the room. And
as I did my best thinking with the rising sun, I let her
talk me to sleep.

But the minute I turned over the next morning, her
voice came back on. "Edith? You sleeping?" She put
on the light. I turned my back. "Oh, I thought you
were awake." I forced my breathing even. But the
light stayed on, and I heard the pages of a book turning.
I kept my back to her.

I tried to think of what she had written me about
Ruby. She had mentioned a dude named Orlando.
Orlando. What had happened? I stretched, yawned,
turned to face Phyllisia.

"Didn't Orlando want to marry Ruby?"

"Who?"

"Orlando."

"Orlando is old stuff. Ruby's boyfriend's name is Manny."

"Manny!"

"Yeah, I wrote you about him." Another of the letters I didn't get. "You'll meet him today. Ruby's invited all her friends. You'd think she was really dying the way she sent out notices."

"Ruby would have had such a pretty baby," I said.

"That we will never know."

"Phyllisia," Ruby called from her room. Phyllisia turned the light off and covered her head. I went in to see Ruby. "What is Phyllisia doing?" she asked.

"Sleeping," I lied.

"Do you mind helping me? I want to go to the bathroom."

I helped Ruby out of bed. Helped her to stand. Let her lean on my shoulders as she went to the bathroom. Her frail body shook; her legs kept giving way. I waited to help her back to bed. And when she got there she collapsed from exhaustion.

Back in Phyllisia's room I started dressing. I didn't understand my friend. "Why do you let Ruby put you on like that?" she asked me. "She's only acting." I didn't look at her. Had Phyllisia always been so selfish?

"Are you mad at me, Edy?" She wanted to know.

"Phyl, Ruby's really sick. She isn't putting on."

"You happy?" she asked, her flat eyes blinking. "Then go on believing."

"Are you making breakfast, Phyllisia?" Ruby called.

"Yes, but you're coming out to get it."

"You don't have to be nasty. Edith will bring it."

Phyllisia put on her robe and stomped into the kitchen. I heard a banging of pots and pans before she finally called, "Come and get it." I did. I prepared Ruby's tray.

On my way to Ruby's room, Phyllisia screamed, "Ayieee! Edy! Edy! Fire! Ohgodohgodohgodohgod. Fire! Fire!" I rushed back to the kitchen to find Phyllisia jumping up and down, up and down. "Help me! Somebody. Help!"

Someone ran past me. Ruby pushed her way into the kitchen. "Where? Where's the fire?" She looked from my puzzled face to Phyllisia's smirking one.

"You ass!" Ruby hissed. "You damn asshole." Without looking at me again, she rushed back to her room.

I brought in her tray anyway. She still didn't look at me. Just lay pouting, tears in her pretty eyes.

Manny came early in the afternoon. Tall, broad, tan-skinned, with curly hair. When he walked in, his big-ness took over. "Hi, princess," he called to Phyllisia. "Where's the queen?"

"One guess." Phyllisia twisted up her mouth. Manny hit her playfully on her head and went toward Ruby's room.

"Wait up, Manny." Phyllisia stopped him. "I want you to meet my friend, Edith."

His eyes passed over me, looked around the room, then came back to me. "Hi," he said, then went on into the bedroom. He hadn't seen me. *He really hadn't seen me. Wiped me out.* I glanced at Phyllisia, wondering if she had noticed. But she was fixing an overturned ashtray on the table, frowning.

The bell rang again. This time three of Ruby's girl friends came in. They were all nice looking. Two of them were tall, with long legs, wearing jeans. The other was tiny, wearing skintight slacks. They were all light-skinned, fashion thin, with soft hair, cut into big Afro hairdos—the envy of every kinky-haired black girl.

They went right to the bedroom when Phyllisia let them in. She stopped them at the door. "Please meet my friend Edith."

They looked around, surprised, then looked at me. The taller two smiled. "Hi," they said together. The tiny one pulled down her mouth at the sides, which made her nose sniff the air. "Your friend? Well, I'll be—" They went into the bedroom.

The skin on my forehead stretched upward as though my eyes were demanding answers. Only I wasn't. I tried to frown it down, but it kept on stretching. They had actually wiped me out. I wanted to be gone. Only I kept sitting. Phyllisia had seen. "Pay those girls no mind, Edy. Ruby always has those fair-skinned girls around her. She thinks they're her friends. But they swear they are better than she."

She didn't have to explain *them* to me. *I knew them.* I had always known them. They had lived around Harlem long before she had come on the scene from the West Indies. They were *Americans like me.*

I had always known those tall, light-skinned, curly-haired Mannys. Marlon Brando fitted better in my dreams.

Those girls with their big Afros—they had always lived around Harlem, somewhere. Their fathers, their mothers had always been our dentists, doctors, lawyers, even our preachers around Harlem. They had walked the streets and never seen me. They had not gone to my schools—no more than whites. They had gone to private schools. Their buses had driven past me while I walked, holes in my stockings, shoes run over, on my way to school. They had never seen me. But I had seen them.

Phyllisia kept talking, but I didn't hear her. I saw her mouth moving, but I didn't hear. I did hear the tiny one screeching from the bedroom, "I tell you those white folks are just going to have to learn how to talk to us blacks."

If they were black, what about me? Clear as anything I heard from the mouth of someone who knew: "You are their statistics."

I went to the window. Looked out. Space. It had to be a dream. This high rise. Me in here with Phyllisia and Ruby. Like spinning through space. Nothing seemed real. Nothing. Why did Phyllisia *see me?* Because we went to school together? Because we had hurt together? Or did she love the habit of loving me? And those, in that room, talking about teaching the white world—were they real?

A few blocks away—no more than five—a man named James had rushed me out of his house, had thrown me into a basement where another man, named Stu, had been kind. I had been hurt. Bruised. That hurt had been real. Seems that my life had exposed me to all kinds of hurt. But none so deep as this. None so deep.

"Edith." Ruby called me into her room after her friends had left. "I'm so happy you came to stay with us." I studied her happy face, so bright, so healthy. I knew she meant that she was glad I had been there to see her friends, see how much they liked her, the attention they paid her.

"I'm not staying, Ruby."

"Why not?"

"I don't belong here."

"You mean because of Mother?"

"No. . . ." I wanted to tell her of my hurt about not being seen. Instead I said, "I'm going to have a baby."

"Oh, Edith. Is that why you left Peekskill?"

"Yes."

"Are you going to marry him?"

"No."

"You don't love him?"

I hitched my shoulders, shook my head. "No."

"How awful. I—I was pregnant—for Manny. But I love him. I really love him."

"Why didn't y'all marry?"

"He wants to finish college. I—I'm going back to

college. I have to study very hard to make it. But I—I'm going back. You see, all my friends go to college."

Just like that I knew why I had felt so close to her, wanted to be near her. Deep in those eyes I saw the mussiness, begging, needing. She reminded me of Bessie! I brushed back her hair; her head nudged my hand. "What are you going to do, Edith?"

"I don't know. Find a job, a place to stay."

"Jobs are so hard to find, Edy. You ought to go to Welfare. It won't take long to get help. And while you're waiting you can stay here."

A flush of resentment started, but Phyllisia came into the room. "What are all you talking about?"

"I just told Ruby that I'm going to have a baby."

"Oh, God, Edith, is true?" Her face lit up. "I'm going to be the godmother."

How did it happen that she stayed so young and I got so old? "How can you be godmother if you running away?" I teased.

"I'll come back," she said. "Nothing can keep me away if you have a baby."

TEN

"Git back here." The young mother sitting next to me grabbed her little son's arm, and in reaching for him, slammed the legs of the baby she held in her arms against me. The boy threw himself on the floor, fighting to get away. "You hear me," she said. "Set back down or I'm gonna slap you so hard you gonna think the sun done set in your nappy head."

The boy kept struggling, and the baby, scared, stiffened and almost fell out of the protecting hook of the mother's elbow. She caught the baby, and the boy, released, ran laughing up the aisle.

Right away a man rushed to take the boy's empty seat. The mother sat back. "Kids ain't nothing but some trouble," she complained. "And these folks in this place act like you don't count 'cause you on Welfare. They figger we all got to wait, right? Wait until time for the damn undertaker."

I didn't answer, but I agreed. I had come at eight-thirty, trying to be first, and my number was eighty-one.

Her little boy running up the aisle had found a friend, then two, then three. They kept up laughing and screaming. Every few minutes the boy came to stand at the end of the row, and his mother shouted, "Come back here, you. Just wait till I get my hand on your butt. I'm gonna make it bubble." Then he ran laughing and screaming back to his friends.

Threats tied them together. If he didn't come to get them, or she wasn't there to give them, they'd both be running wild, scared out of their minds.

God, I hated sitting there waiting. But what did you do if you needed help? An unwed mother-to-be, unemployed, who used to belong to The Institution. That meant automatic Welfare. No problem. In a little while I'd have me a place—a room—and be no trouble to a living soul.

The mother leaned against me, pushing me onto the fat, hot woman sitting next to me. The woman heaved her shoulders. I straightened up. It happened again. The next time, the fat woman turned on me. "Don't you do that to me. Do you hear? Don't you do that to me."

I heard her. I got up. Gave the girl my seat. The dude sitting next to her had fallen asleep—nodding. Each time he fell against her, she had pushed me. She kept jabbing him with her elbow, trying to keep him awake.

I stood along the wall of the packed room, filled with mostly blacks and Puerto Ricans, and a handful of whites. I kept looking at the fat woman. Heard again what she had said to me: "Listen," she had said. "I worked hard in this life. Struggled. I got to stand everything, from everybody. But the next push, from you or anybody, will be one push too much."

"Numbers seventy-eight, seventy-nine, eighty, eighty-one. Go to Section C."

I joined the group, went to Section C, and sat again, waiting. The mother with her two children sat next to me again.

This time, tired and hungry, the little boy wanted her attention. He kept shaking her, and she kept trying to feed the baby. "Quit it, you hear? If you don't quit I'll break every finger in them hands." The boy snatched the bottle from the baby's mouth and stuck it into his. The mother struggled with him. He held on. The baby screamed.

I broke down. "I'll feed the baby."

Grateful, she handed over the baby and picked up the little boy to give him his bottle. I loosened the blankets from around the hot baby, took off the woolen cap from her sweaty head. God, what a shame folks having babies and not knowing how to care for them. She looked younger than me. Like she had started before having the time to dream.

I closed my eyes to think about that one. Folks dreaming. All I had ever had were nightmares. Folks like Ruby and Bessie dreamed from need. Searching, looking for things to grab hold to. They found it and took off. Folks like Phyllisia dreamed to be dreaming. It kept her young. Next year this time she'd still be dreaming of running away unless a new, exciting dream slid into its place.

I put the baby over my shoulder to burp and looked across to the other section where a tall, light-skinned girl with a big Afro hairdo sat reading. I kept looking at her. She didn't belong. Everyone else in the place did—even the whites with their straggly hair, their pulled-together look, their down talk, all a part of belonging.

But this chick looked out of it. Weird. Folks all around kept staring at her. Me too. She kept reading— or more like it, her head was bent toward a book. She never turned one page. I gave the baby another chance at the bottle and kept looking at the chick to see if she'd ever reach the end of the page.

"Seventy-six, seventy-seven—"

The chick stood up and followed the interviewer. She walked tall, straight as a board, head high, not seeing us. Not wanting to be seen by us. But every eye followed her out of the room. *"You don't see us. But we see you."*

Now she needed help, and she had to come to the same place we had.

"We?" Words catch. We? Who we? The statistics, of course. Her statistics, the part that is added and subtracted to make a point. The faceless ones. The needy. But *she needed*. So why did our eyes follow her as though she was an enemy?

She carried herself that way. She thought that *we* were the enemy! To be in this place and to be thought one of *us* shamed her. Shamed her to her soul!

My mind flipped. Back to my old man, shuffling out of the door and never coming back, a statistic; Randy, shot by a cop, a statistic; Ellen dead, malnutrition, a statistic; Bessie dead, a statistic; Suzy, missing person, a statistic. Minnie . . .

Naw, Minnie Cramer was brilliant, special. She had known what she wanted. She had made a choice. She had an address, a name that counted.

And I had resented her, my baby sister. I had known where to see her and I hadn't gone. Hadn't wanted to see her. Now I still knew where she was. But more, Suzy knew where she was. Fun—ny. Minnie Cramer had become the line to keep our family in touch.

I thought of things I resented: Mrs. Ortiz at The Institution, for saying I should work as an attendant; the doorman at Phyllisia's for his attitude; Manny and those other friends of Ruby's for not seeing me; Ruby for saying to me, *"I can't have a baby. I have to go to college."* And in the next breath she said, *"You are having a baby. You can get Welfare."*

The baby in my arms pushed her bottle away. She smiled. I felt sad for her. *What are you doing here, li'l girl? Why are so many of you here, hanging around the Welfare, orphan homes, foster homes? The Institutions? What did you do to rate it? What did Mary Allen do? What did Pip-Squeak do?*

" Seventy-eight, seventy-nine."

"That's me." The mother snatched her baby from me, tried to wake the boy, who had fallen asleep, gave up, pushed him under one arm, grabbed the baby bag, and rushed off. I looked at her as she went. Kept looking at the space through which she disappeared.

How did folks like her, all burdened down, get a face on? How did she get to be seen? How did folks like me get to count? A straightening fact: it took a lifetime of work—and someone in your corner besides.

"Eighty, eighty-one."

I got up to follow the social worker but found myself walking, walking. I walked out of the building and through the streets until I found a telephone booth. Went in. Dialed. Waited.

"Yes?"

"Mrs.—Moms?"

A long silence. "Edith? Are you at the station?" I could see her fingering her pearls.

"No'm. I—I'm in New York."

"Do you want to tell me why you left?"

"I—I—I'm having a baby."

"Ooooh?"

"I—I—for James. . . ."

A silence. Then she said, "I—I do make mistakes, don't I?"

How did she mean that? My heart thumped. Did she mean she had made a mistake with me? That she had changed her mind about me? That she no longer wanted to help me help myself? I was on my own? Did I have to go it alone?

"Where are you staying?"

"With my friend Phyllisia."

"What are your plans?"

"I—I'm going to have an abortion."

"Good idea. Do you want me with you?"

'Yes'm."

"Good. I'll drive right down. What is her address?"

ABOUT THE AUTHOR

ROSA GUY was born in Trinidad, raised in Harlem, and is a founder of the Harlem Writers Guild.

With *Edith Jackson*, Ms. Guy completes a trilogy that explores the mutability of family and personal relationships in black society today, especially among women. The first of these books, *The Friends*, was named by the American Library Association as one of the Best of the Best books published in the last fifteen years of particular interest to young people. *Ruby*, the second book in the trilogy, was selected as a Best Book for Young Adults by the ALA.

The author of two other books, Ms. Guy lives in New York City and is at work on her next novel.

00-1
63-1